PS: It Was Murder

Ashleigh Stevens

This is a work of fiction. Names, characters, businesses, places, events, locales, and incidents are either the products of the author's imagination or used in a fictitious manner. Any resemblance to actual persons, living or dead, or actual events is purely coincidental.

PS: IT WAS MURDER

First edition. 2023

Copyright © Ashleigh Stevens.

All rights reserved

Kindle ISBN: 9781957741055

Paperback ISBN: 9781957741048

Library of Congress Control Number: 2023904346

Edited by

Work In Progress Wonders

www.WIPWonders.com

Other Works by Ashleigh Stevens

Young Adults
Camp Piquaqua
Elephant on my Chest

Hartfield Chronicles
Lesson 0: A New Home
Lesson 1: Adjusting to a New Life
Webserial

Romances
Kayaks, Kisses & Monsters
Mooncrossed

Mysteries
PS: It Was Murder
One Night In Sedona (writing as Carrie Latimer)

To receive updates on new releases, visit
www.AshleighStevensBSB.com
or join my newsletter
https://ashleighstevens.eo.page/whodunit

August 20, 1991

Dear Lisa,

Hi! I'm Katie and I was matched with you for the Girls Only Magazine Pen pal thing. I am really excited. I've never had a pen pal before. Have you?

Anyway. I'm 11 years old and I live in Pinewood, Connecticut. It's a little town on Long Island Sound. We can walk to the beach from my house.

What else? I have a 9-year-old brother. He can be sooooo annoying sometimes! But at least next week we won't be going to the same school anymore. Because I'm starting middle school! It's like junior high, except this year the 9th grade is moving to the high school and the 6th grade will be at the junior high now. Strange, huh? But we go for a tour tomorrow. So I'll tell you all about it in my next letter.

I better go. I can't wait to hear from you.

Your new pen pal,
Katie Winters

August 25, 1991

Dear Katie,

I can't believe it! I was about to write to you when I got your letter in the mail. How awesome that we are already thinking alike. I just know we're going to be good friends.

You asked a lot of questions. No, I've never had a pen pal before. I'm 11 too! When's your birthday? Mine is June 4th. It's cool that you're near the beach. I live in Copper Cove, Maine. Well, I guess you know that, since you sent me a letter. Anyway, it's on the coast, but we have to drive about 15 minutes to get to the beach. But there's a cool lighthouse near my house. I can ride my bike there if Jeff comes with me.

That's right. I have a brother, too, but he's 13. Our school is a little different from yours. We have kindergarten to eighth grade. So, Jeff's still in my school.

Do you have any hobbies? I love to read. Mysteries are my favorite. I also like creating my own stories. I hope to be a writer when I grow up. How about you? What do you want to be when you grow up?

Oh. My mom is calling me for dinner. I better go. Write back soon!

Your friend,
Lisa

September 15, 1994
From: KatieWinters@cttc.net
To: lgardner@downeast.net

Dear Lisa,

Can you believe it? We FINALLY got a computer! I am so glad you told me your email address. We just got it today. My brother wants to play some weird mine game on it, but my mom said we each get one hour. And I have so much to tell you!

First of all, I was so happy to hear about you and Brad. That is so sweet that your lockers are near each other. How are things going with you guys? What do you do together? You know I've never had a boyfriend. Do you hang out at each other's houses? I know a lot of the couples at my school sit together at lunch. Do you guys? Have you kissed him yet? What's it like? None of my other friends have kissed a boy yet, so no one has been able to tell me.

Speaking of boys, remember that boy who wouldn't stop annoying me last year? Brian? He's in ALL my classes this year. And, I don't know about your school, but in ours, the bell is always ringing. And I jump out of my seat every time. Literally. Every. Single. Time. And Brian is always the first one to laugh at me.

But it's not all bad. There's this cute boy Chris in my geometry class. He's a sophomore, and he sits next to me. He keeps asking to borrow my notes. I can't tell if he likes me or not. I was thinking of writing him a note. What do you think?

Oh, no. My time's almost up. I'm going to need to learn to type faster. Write back soon.

Love,
Katie

September 16, 1994
From: lgardner@downeast.net
To: katiewinters@cttc.net

Dear Katie,

I am so excited you got a computer. Now we can write, like, every day. It gives me a chance to say: DON'T LEAVE CHRIS A NOTE! That is so 8th grade. We're mature high school women now. Send him an email.

Just kidding. You should ask him to study for a test together, like at the library after school. Or do homework or something. Then, while you're at the library, you make a casual comment like, "Your girlfriend must hate that you're studying instead of spending time with her" and wait for his reaction. If he doesn't have a girlfriend, there's a chance he'll show some sign he's interested in you.

Of course, I have no idea what I'm talking about, but that's my plan for the heroine in my latest story. Stacey is going to ask a boy to study with her and she'll say something like that. I haven't figured out what will happen. Should they kiss? Should he have a girlfriend? Or maybe the monster should attack before Stacey even finds out whether he's single.

In real life, Brad and I live in different towns, so we mostly only see each other at school. We talk on the phone almost every night, though. I keep asking my parents to let me get my own phone line, like Brad has, but they keep saying no. But Jeff is on the computer so much, we're going to get a second line for the modem. My parents said they will consider connecting that number to my room. It's not exactly a private line, but it's something.

Speaking of annoying older brothers, it's his turn. He's just going to spend his hour playing some mine game. I bet it's the same one your brother plays.

Write back soon. I want to know how things go with Chris.

Love,
Lisa

KTGurl98: Are you around?

Mysterista: Agh! I can't believe I finally caught you online. How was rush week?

KTGurl98: I decided not to rush. I looked at all the sororities, but I couldn't really picture myself in any of them. Just didn't feel right, you know? Maybe next year. How's Bridgewater?

Mysterista: So fantastic. My creative writing teacher is amazing. He has all these incredible ideas. I have learned so much already.

KTGurl98: Awesome. My classes have been pretty boring. I got a C on my bio test. Questioning the whole med-school thing.

Mysterista: I thought you had your heart set on being a doctor

KTGurl98: There's this cool program here where we volunteer once a week at the local ER. We're just walking around with a clipboard doing a survey about whether people got the flu shot this year. But, it's spending four hours a week in the ER.

Mysterista: That's good, right?

KTGurl98: Kind of. I saw these women come in after an accident. They were in rough shape. Another time, an old guy had a heart attack, and they couldn't save him. And, well, I realized I don't want to be responsible for other people's lives.

Mysterista: Well, good thing you figured that out before wasting 4 years in med school.

KTGurl98: hehe

Mysterista: So, now what? Are you staying bio?

KTGurl98: For now. Until I figure out what I want to do.

Mysterista: Any ideas?

KTGurl98: Well, I'd love to do jigsaw puzzles all day. But I doubt I can make a living from that.

Mysterista: hehe. That would be so cool. Oh! I gotta go. I've got class in 10 minutes on the other side of campus.

KTGurl98: Have fun! Talk to you soon!

July 7, 2003

Dear Lisa,

I hope you get this letter. I wasn't sure where else to send it. I don't have the address of your new apartment, but I figured your family would know where to find you.

How is everything? I haven't heard from you in a while. I tried emailing you and left a few voicemails, but you never got back to me, and now your voice mailbox is full. Hopefully, you've just been busy.

How is the writing coming? I read that chapter you emailed me. It was fantastic, but I'm dying to read more. I think you may have a bestseller on your hands.

Anyway, I'm still working at the coffee shop, trying to figure out what to do with my life. Remember when I said I wanted to do jigsaw puzzles all day? Is that still an option?

Well, I hope things are okay with you and that I haven't heard from you because you're so busy working on your novel. I really hope you're not ignoring me because you're mad at me. (If you are, please tell me what I did?)

Write back soon. (Or better yet, call me!)

Love,
Katie

July 14, 2003

Dear Katie,

I can't tell you how happy I was to see your letter. I have been trying to track you down, but there are so many Katie Winterses in Connecticut that I didn't know where to look. Lisa has told me a lot about you over the years and I know you were her best friend, so I didn't want to ignore your letter.

Has Lisa ever told you about Lighthouse Point? There's a jetty where a lot of us like to go watch the waves. And the fishermen. At low tide, you can walk along the rocks, but they can be kind of slippery.

Anyway, back in April, Lisa was out at Lighthouse Point. Fishermen found her tangled in some of their lobster pots and, well, we think she must have slipped while walking along the jetty.

As you know, she was the only family I had left. Losing her has been difficult. But I find some comfort knowing she has moved on to a better place.

I'm sorry you thought Lisa was mad at you. She left me no way to contact you. But I know you meant a lot to her and, well, I guess she can rest in peace now that you know what happened.

Sincerely,
Jeff Gardner

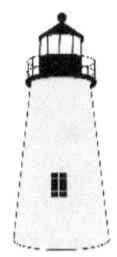

Chapter 1

I STARED AT THE LETTER IN MY HAND. I HAD read it more times than I could count, but it still made no sense. How could my oldest friend be dead?

Maybe the note wasn't real. I rushed to my computer. Did Copper Cove have a local newspaper?

According to Jeeves, it did. They even published its articles online. I typed in Lisa's name and received two hits. A story more or less summarizing what Jeff had said. Local fishermen had discovered my friend the first week in April.

The only other article was Lisa's obituary, listing her brother as her sole surviving relative. It was a little sad, actually. He hadn't even given her a funeral. Only a graveside memorial.

And I had missed it.

I glanced at the calendar hanging on my wall. It had been nearly four months since her death. Was it too late to pay my respects?

I jumped to my feet, running to the front door of my studio apartment. Late was better than never. I had my keys in my hand, fingers on the knob, when I remembered that Copper Cove was nearly five hours away. Besides, I had no idea how to get there.

With a sigh, I threw my keys in the basket and flopped on my bed. This was going to take a little more planning. I would visit Lisa tomorrow.

"WHAT DO YOU MEAN, YOU NEED SOME TIME OFF?"

Hefting a sack of espresso beans, I followed my boss out of the back room. "My friend passed away. I need to pay my respects."

Todd frowned. "How long will you be gone?"

I placed the beans on the counter with a sigh. "I dunno. A couple days?"

While Todd considered this information, I opened the bag, inhaling the rich scent and scooping beans into the hopper. When the bag was about half empty, I was able to lift it to pour in the rest. A sound like glass breaking echoed across the coffee shop, and a few patrons looked to see what was happening. But most kept to themselves.

Todd frowned as I closed the hopper. "You can take this week. I'll get Jen to cover for you. But I need you back by next Saturday."

I nodded. "Thanks, Todd. This means a lot to me."

Shaking his head, my boss turned to the customer behind the register. I spent the rest of my shift watching the clock. As soon as the hour hand settled on the one, I whipped off my apron and punched my time card.

My suitcase was waiting for me in the back room. I felt a little silly dragging it through town. Especially since I kept bumping into tourists. A few people gave me a peculiar look or two, but I trudged on. The full mile to Eddie's garage, on the edge of downtown.

I drummed my fingers on the counter while I waited for his wife to get off the phone. In the five years I had been bringing Cindi to this shop, I had yet to learn her name.

Mrs. Eddie hung up the phone, turning to me with a smile. "Hi, dearie. How can I help you?"

"I'm here to pick up my Tracker? Katie Winters?"

She rifled through the stack of papers on her desk. "Winters. Winters. Ah, yes. Here you are. That will be $176.78."

"For what? You were supposed to fix the brakes."

"Yes, dearie. But you needed new rotors. It says here Eddie discussed this with you yesterday."

I sighed. "Yeah. I just didn't realize it would be so expensive." I handed over my debit card.

After running it through the machine, Mrs. Eddie returned the card along with my keys. "All set, Dearie. You'll see it in front."

I waited until I was out of Rockland before stopping at a gas station. Not that prices were much better inland, but at least they weren't over a dollar a gallon. After filling the tank, I ran inside, purchasing a soda and bag of chips from the mini-mart. As an afterthought, I grabbed some peanuts and chocolate-covered raisins for protein. Five hours was a long drive.

Provisions in hand, I pulled out the directions I had printed last night. After propping them on the seat beside me, I turned on the radio and headed north.

A couple of hours later, my soda was long gone, and I needed a restroom. Of course, there were none in sight. I settled for listening to my music.

I hadn't bothered making a road trip playlist. My CD collection was sufficient, even if the player did skip every time I went over a bump. At least I had the adaptor so I could listen to it in the car's cassette stereo. Lisa had told me she was driving with headphones on to listen to CDs in her car.

I was wondering how far it was to the next bathroom when my Discman ran out of batteries. Ejecting the adapter from the cassette player, I fumbled with the radio, finding a top 40 station as I crossed the Maine border.

Half an hour later, I pulled into a rest stop. People sent me sidelong glances as I rushed to the ladies' room.

But I didn't care. I had been in that car for over two hours and had consumed a very large soda.

Apparently, I wasn't the only one. Three other women were doing potty dances similar to mine while waiting in line in front of me. After five excruciating minutes, it was my turn.

When I emerged from the restroom, I examined the large map near the front door. The state of Maine was bigger than my head. I was in the bottom left corner. I searched along the coast for Copper Cove. It wasn't there.

But I saw Kensington, and that sounded familiar. Wasn't that where Lisa had gone to high school or something? I traced Route 49 south with my finger. At the very tip of a peninsula, I found it. Copper Cove.

It was near the center of the map, on the coast, of course. I had barely crossed the border. I sighed. Maine was a lot bigger than Connecticut. I still had a long way to go.

Although they were horribly overpriced, I bought fresh batteries at the convenience store. I needed music to get me through this incredibly long journey. After grabbing a burger and fries from the fast-food place, I returned to my car, topping off my tank before setting out on the second half of my journey.

I wasn't on the highway for very long. By the time I finished my meal, I was pulling onto Route 1. But being on the back roads made the journey feel that much longer. Every few minutes, I was stopping for a red light. After passing through a town, I could accelerate. The road went over a bridge connecting two peninsulas and traffic again slowed. This pattern continued for more than an hour. Finally, after changing my CD twice, I spotted the turnoff for the coastal route.

I was almost there. According to my directions, I only had a mile on this road, then another fifteen on the local ones. I was so close to Lisa, I could taste it.

Except the traffic on the coastal route slowed to a crawl. No one seemed to want to go anywhere. It took over thirty minutes to inch my way half a mile to what I assumed was the center of town. It reminded me of where I worked. Boutiques and restaurants geared to the summer travelers. Seafood and lobster everywhere. Docks to eat outside.

It was also filled with the same tourists. Pedestrians flooded the sidewalks. Jaywalkers forced the cars in the road to stop abruptly, much like waiting for a family of geese to cross the street. Except, the birds would have been faster.

Eventually, I made it through the center and turned onto Route 49. The sun was setting on my right as I drove away from the town. Houses became more spread out. I saw a few farms, but mostly trees.

Lisa had tried to describe this to me. She had even sent me a few pictures, but I had never fully understood her rural life. I had grown up in suburbia with people crowded on top of each other and claiming they had space. It was peaceful here. The perfect place for her to write her novel.

I glanced at my directions. I was looking for Lupine Street on my right. It was difficult to see the signs. Although most of the traffic had gone, I drove like a senior citizen. I kept slowing at every minor intersection to read the signs.

And yet, I still missed Lupine Street. I drove all the way to a lighthouse at the end of the road. I planned on turning around in the parking lot, but the welcome sign made a lump form in my throat. This wasn't just any lighthouse.

It was Lighthouse Point. Where Lisa had died.

I sat in my car for a while, opening the windows and listening to the waves crash against the shore. I could see the jetty from here. An outcropping of rocks protruding into the ocean like a gnarled finger.

People were sitting on the rocks. Most were near the shore, but some had made their way to the tip. What were they thinking? Didn't they know how dangerous that was? That a girl had died only a few months ago from doing the same thing?

As I climbed out of my car, I glanced at the license plates around me. New Hampshire. Massachusetts. Even New Brunswick and Nova Scotia. No. These people probably didn't know my best friend had died.

On my way to the water, I passed a field of wildflowers. Lavender cones were growing among small white and yellow blooms. I picked a few of each kind to create a little bouquet as I made my way to the jetty.

Judging by the waterline on the damp rocks, the tide was going out. Did that make the area safer? Had Lisa fallen at low tide because the rocks were wet and slippery? Or high tide because the waves had swept her away?

I walked to the edge of the grass, to a cliff on the right of the jetty. There were fewer people here. Most were on the other side, closer to the lighthouse.

A gentle breeze ruffled my hair as I settled in the grass and stared at the rocks. Listening to the waves, I thought about my best friend. Lisa had sat here only a few short months ago. I knew how much she had loved Lighthouse Park. When she wasn't away at school, she would come here at least once a week. It was one of her favorite writing places. She had found it peaceful.

I wasn't sure I agreed. The kids on the rocks were pretty loud. Although, the surf did almost drown them out.

However, as I watched the waves crashing against the jetty, the surrounding noises slowly abated. The surf was mesmerizing. And peaceful. I could see why Lisa loved it here.

With a sigh, I wiped a tear from the corner of my eye. "I miss you, Lisa."

Even though I was whispering, my voice sounded loud. I glanced around, but no one had heard me. I was alone. When had they all left? How long had I been lost in thought?

I turned back to the water. Lisa had been happy here. Hopefully, no matter what had caused her to fall, she had at least died happy.

The sun was disappearing over the horizon. I had hoped to find the cemetery before losing daylight. With a sigh, I got to my feet, wiping my other eye.

After placing my bouquet on the passenger's seat, I started the car. Would I have enough daylight left to find the cemetery?

And then what? As I pulled back onto the road, I realized I hadn't passed any hotels. The occasional bed-and-breakfast, but they all had *No Vacancy* signs. Where was I going to sleep tonight?

I shook my head. One problem at a time.

It took me ten minutes, but I eventually found Lupine Street. As soon as I turned, I kept my eyes peeled for the cemetery. It appeared on a bluff overlooking the ocean. There was no parking lot, so I pulled along the side of the road. Since I was losing daylight, I reached under my seat for my heavy-duty flashlight to help me see the markers. After grabbing my bouquet, I went in search of my friend.

A knee-high wrought-iron fence separated the cemetery from the road. Why? What could it possibly keep out? Moose could jump it. Squirrels could run under it. I could step over it.

I scanned the stone crosses and angels, but the people closest to the road had died before the second world war. Heading between them, I crept closer to the water. I needed my flashlight to read the engravings. But the dates on the stones grew older and older until I was staring at graves from the 1830s.

Now what? According to Jeeves, this was the only cemetery in the entire town. If Lisa wasn't here, then where was she?

Before I could figure it out, a bright light blinded me. I automatically raised my hands to shield my eyes as someone behind the light spoke.

"I saw your car on the side of the road. Is everything okay?" The deep voice was definitely male and held a tone of concern. It didn't belong to the local sheriff, right? Suddenly, I felt like I was trespassing.

I frowned. "Not really. I came to pay my respects to a friend and now someone is blinding me with a flashlight."

The man gave a small laugh as he moved the light to my feet. "Well, unless you're a lot older than you look, I doubt you're going to find your friend in here."

I blinked a few times until the spot blinding my vision faded. The man didn't look that much older than me. And I was pretty sure he wasn't the police, unless jeans and a t-shirt were what they were wearing nowadays. I glanced behind him. Even a small-town sheriff would most likely drive something better than the beat-up pickup truck parked behind my Tracker.

The man waved the flashlight in a small circle. "It's getting late. Maybe we can find your friend in the morning?"

Nodding, I took a hesitant step toward the road. The man moved between two stones, using his flashlight to indicate I should go first. I passed him with a frown.

"What are you, the cemetery police?"

"No. But, I am a member of the Copper Cove Historical Society. And the Copper Cove Community Council."

While I didn't think that was a real association, I held my tongue. We had reached my car. When his light landed on my license plate, he froze, glancing from me to the car a few times. But it was too dark to read his expression.

After a moment, he jerked his head, swinging the flashlight toward the road. "Come on. Let's go visit your friend."

What had he seen to change his mind so quickly?

He crossed to the opposite side of the street, continuing along it until he reached the crest of a hill. I bit my lip. Was I supposed to follow him? For all I knew, he could be some crazy ax murderer leading me to my death. Although, the only weapon I saw in his hand was a flashlight, and I had one of those as well. Besides, he seemed too good-looking to be a crazed killer.

Night had fallen, and I only knew where the man was because of his light. I followed the speck. There was another cemetery here. The markers closest to the road were from around World War II. I stepped over another low fence, weaving through graves until I caught up to the man.

He had stopped moving, kneeling beside a marker in the back of the cemetery. The grass wasn't as full here. Someone had been buried recently.

As I approached, the man got to his feet, gesturing to the grave. "I'm guessing this is who you were looking for?"

I shined my light on the stone.

Lisa Brooke Gardner
Born: June 4, 1980
Died: April 25, 2003

My breath caught. I had found her.

Stacey opened the newspaper with a sigh. How on earth was she going to find a research topic when everything was so depressing?

There was war in the Middle East. Sure, she would be able to find a plethora of information. And put both her professor and herself to sleep in the process.

The presidential candidates were having a debate. Stacey could write her entire research paper on their platforms alone. Educational reform. Foreign policy. Global warming. Boring, boring, boring.

She wanted something fresh. Something no one else in her class would be doing. Something like the brief article on the bottom of page six.

A student had been found dead in the quad. Authorities believed she had OD'd after a frat party.

Many people overdosed on campus each year. Sure, not all of them died, but a lot did. Enough to be the topic of a research paper? Stacey wasn't sure.

But she was going to find out.

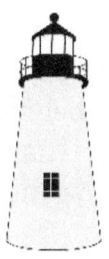

Chapter 2

I PLACED MY FLOWERS AT THE BASE OF THE GRAVE marker, running a hand along the smooth stone. Until this moment, part of me had held onto the belief that Lisa might not be dead. I wanted to say something, anything, but a lump had formed in my throat. Tears blurred my eyes and my knees buckled.

The strange man was by my side in a heartbeat, grabbing my arm in one hand and wrapping his other around my waist. "Katie? You okay?"

I nodded, trying to take a deep breath as the man eased me to the ground.

"I'll give you a few minutes. If you need anything, I'll be right here."

He gestured to his side. Lisa's grave was near the right edge of the cemetery. While the man went to sit on the low fence, I let the tears stream down my cheeks.

"Oh, Lisa. It's not fair. What am I going to do without you? Who's going to help me with questions about boys? You were supposed to help me figure out what to do with my life. And what about your book? You were so close to finishing it. You were going to be a famous author."

I turned away from the guy on the fence so he wouldn't see me wipe my tears with the cuff of my sleeve. Out of the corner of my eye, I saw motion. Glancing in that direction, I realized it was moonlight playing on the water. The bluff looked into a bay. I turned back to Lisa.

"You have a lovely view. I'm going to have to come visit you more often." Getting to my feet, I turned to the man with a sniffle, gesturing behind me weakly. "I'm, uh, gonna head back to my car. Thanks for showing me where Lisa was." I frowned. "How did you know she was the friend I was visiting?"

He got to his feet with a laugh, falling into step beside me as we made our way down the hill. "It was a pretty safe bet. Lisa was the only person in Copper Cove who has passed away in eight months. Before her was Mrs. Hawkes. She was eighty-three years old, and no one liked her."

I continued down the hill in silence, admiring both the view in front of me and the one beside me while listening to an amazing symphony. Waves crashed rhythmically below us, providing a percussion to the insect orchestra. Every so often, I would catch the howling solo of a creature I couldn't identify.

I turned to the man as we approached our cars. "Is that a wolf?"

He cocked his head, listening a moment before shaking it. "The loons."

"That's what they sound like? Lisa was always mentioning them, but I never heard one before."

"So, do you need directions back to wherever you're staying? Or do you know your way around?"

I bit my lip. "Actually, if you could point me to a hotel—"

The guy's laughter echoed in the quiet night. "A hotel. That's a good one. We have some B and B's around, but this time of year, they're usually all booked. You don't have a place to stay?"

I shrugged. "It's no big deal. I can just go into the next town."

The man shook his head. "The closest hotel is in Trussboro, which is almost an hour away. Why don't you stay at my place? There are a few things I want to show you."

The alarm bells ringing in my head drowned out the birdsong. "Yeah, uh, not happening. I don't go home with strangers." I quickly climbed into my car, locking the doors, though with the roof off, there was probably no point.

The guy laughed. "That's a good one. Come on, Katie. You're practically family. If Lisa were alive, she'd make you stay. You know she would."

Yeah, she would. She had, the handful of times I had visited her at her college. But how did this guy know that? Come to think of it—

"How do you know my name?"

He gestured to my car. "Connecticut plates. Who else would be looking for Lisa a week after I sent you a letter telling you she had passed?" He extended his hand to me. "I'm Lisa's brother. Jeff Gardner."

I didn't shake his hand. This guy couldn't be Jeff. Lisa's brother was an annoying thirteen-year-old boy who was always looking for his sister's diary and hogging the computer. In my head, he was a lot like my younger brother.

Except, my brother wasn't so little anymore, was he? He was in college. According to Lisa, Jeff had graduated a few years ago and was a history teacher at their old high school. Could this gorgeous man standing before me be my best friend's brother?

I frowned. "How do I know you're really who you say you are?"

Shaking his head, he reached into his back pocket, opening his wallet to show me his driver's license. Jeff Gardner. 15 Pheasant Lane. Copper Cove, Maine. The picture matched the guy in front of me.

I sighed. "Okay. Yeah. I guess I could stay at your place tonight."

"Great." He climbed into his truck, the roaring engine echoing in the quiet night. A moment later, he passed me so quickly that he was over the crest of the hill before I had even started the ignition. How was I supposed to follow him if I couldn't see him?

I hurried down the hill, keeping an eye open for his truck. I saw nothing. Between the moonlight and my headlights, I was able to discern the occasional house, usually dark. After many twists and turns, the street ended at a stop sign. Jeff's pickup was waiting for me. A few roads later, we were pulling onto Pheasant Lane, into the first driveway on the right.

A two-story clapboard house stood at the end of the winding gravel path. Like many of the homes I had passed this afternoon, the wood had faded to nearly gray, darkened with age. Yet the screened porch with white wicker furniture looked comfortable. Although I had never been here before, the place felt warm and inviting.

Jeff pulled behind the house to a detached garage. As he waited for the door to open, he stuck his head out his window.

"You can park here. I'll be right out."

I nodded, pulling beside him as the double door reached its peak. My headlights shone on the baby blue 1968 Volkswagen Beetle backed into the second space. I recognized it immediately as Lisa's graduation present from her parents. Even though it was older than us, she had kept it in mint condition. A lump formed in my throat as a memory bubbled to the surface. Lisa pulling up to my Boston dorm in her bug. An impromptu trip to the Cape. Sunbathing in the last vestiges of summer as we swapped stories about our first week of college.

As the garage door closed, swallowing Lisa's car, my memory faded. I returned to the present as Jeff appeared by my window. "You okay?"

I nodded. "Yeah. I was just . . ." I didn't bother trying to make an excuse. Frowning, I glanced at the sky. "I should probably put the roof back on."

"Want a hand?"

I had done it myself a million times, but there was something about Jeff's smile that I couldn't resist. "That would be great."

While I climbed onto my seat, he walked around to the other side of the truck. "I don't actually know how to do this."

I laughed. "It's not hard. Watch."

I reached into the back seat, pulling the roll bar on the side before straightening. Standing in the sunroof, I started unrolling the canvas, with Jeff assisting me from the side of the car. I grabbed the two nylon straps and tugged, pulling the rest of the roof into place before passing one to Jeff and pointing to a spot just above the passenger door.

"So, this should snap in right over here."

After doing the same on the driver's side, I pulled up the bar in the front and turned to Jeff. "Can you hold this upright? This part is a little tricky."

He looked confused, but did as I asked. After pulling the canvas as close to me as possible, I ducked while throwing it over the bar, emerging on the other side. I snapped the canvas onto the underside before climbing out of the car. I looked at Jeff through the passenger window.

"Okay. So, this is the tricky part. Slowly bring the roof down. It's really taut and will break, so you have to go slow."

I tried not to cringe when his definition of slow was faster than mine, but the roof didn't crack. I climbed into the car to lock the front bar back in place, then opened the passenger door.

"Think you can roll up the window for me? And lock it?"

He shrugged. "Sure."

After doing the same on the driver's side, I opened the tailgate. The rear windows were in the little pouch I had installed on the door. I zipped the passenger one in place, sliding it into the tracks before closing it the rest of the way and securing the self-adhesive fastenings, both inside and out.

As I moved to repeat the procedure on the opposite window, I saw Jeff's raised eyebrows. "What?"

He shrugged. "Seems like a lot of work. Wouldn't you rather have a car with power windows?"

I waited until the window was secure before turning back to him. "Wasn't available for this girl. And I've been in love with this since I was fourteen."

I pulled my bags from the trunk before zipping closed the rear window. After checking my keys were in my pocket, I locked the tailgate and shut the door.

"Okay. All set."

Jeff made a show of checking his watch. "Power windows. Just saying."

I rolled my eyes. "Are we going inside? Or should I sleep in my truck tonight?"

"That's not a truck."

Jeff grabbed my suitcase, lifting it with ease. Not that it was all that heavy. I followed him through a back door into a spacious kitchen. Setting my bag on the floor, he gestured to a large table on the right.

"Hungry?"

I frowned. "I wasn't. But yeah. Now I am."

He opened the side-by-side refrigerator with a laugh. "How long was your drive?"

"Six, seven hours?"

"I hoped you stopped."

"Just for a quick burger."

When Jeff closed the fridge, his arms were laden with glass baking dishes. He put them on a nearby counter, lifting one to peer inside. "Okay. So, we have a tuna noodle casserole. I don't actually recommend this one."

Frowning, he placed the dish in the sink before picking up the next one. "Baked chicken with green beans. That was fantastic. Or beef stroganoff. Good, not great."

"They both sound fine to me."

Jeff removed the glass covers from the dishes. "There's only a little left of each. I'll make both. We can share."

Returning the lids, he placed them in the oven, turned the knob, and pulled two plates from a nearby cabinet. "Beer or water?"

I sighed. "Beer would be great. I can get it."

He gestured to a dorm-sized fridge sitting on the counter beside the regular one. "Drinks are in there."

I raised my eyebrows as I stood. "Why do you have two fridges?"

He shrugged. "This one's like new. Didn't want to get rid of it after college. Gives me more room in the big one."

How much food did a single guy need? My fridge was smaller than his and usually empty. Shaking my head, I examined the contents of the smaller fridge. "You actually drink this stuff?"

"Hey. There's nothing wrong with the cheap stuff."

"You want a list?"

He opened a cabinet next to the oven. "I think I have . . . Yup. This any better?"

He held up a bottle of Lisa's favorite beer, a local lager. I nodded, unable to speak with the lump in my throat. Jeff also seemed to be at a loss for words. He wordlessly removed one of his own beers from the fridge, as well as two frosted glass mugs from the freezer. Popping the caps of each bottle, he poured the drinks. His was a pale yellow that looked, and probably tasted, like something that should go directly into the toilet. Mine was a deep amber that smelled delicious.

I closed my eyes, taking a cautious sip, and was transported in time.

I WAS LOUNGING ON A LOW CHAIR ON THE beach, my beer concealed in a bright pink cozy so the sweat wouldn't attract a pound of sand. Before me, waves crashed gently on the shore. Beside me, Lisa was sipping from a green cozy.

"Can you believe we're graduating this year?"

I groaned. "I still have no idea what I'm going to do with my life, Lis."

"Apply to grad school like me."

Sipping my drink, I shook my head. "And study what? I'm not paying for another four years of school if I don't know what I'm doing."

She held her bottle toward the surf. "You can study marine biology."

I frowned. "No. Most of my classes have been micro. If I go to grad school, it would be to work in a lab. And I tried that this summer. I was miserable. I never got to see the sun."

Lisa giggled. "You are so pasty. You're going to burn this weekend."

I rolled my eyes. "Not all of us were paid to sit outside and write all summer. I hope you finished that manifesto."

"It's not a manifesto. It's a novel. And yes, it's done."

I sat upright, looking at her with wide eyes. "It is? Why didn't you tell me?"

She shrugged. "I finished it the other day. I haven't even typed it all out. It's mostly still in my notebook. But I don't like it."

I flopped back into my chair. "So, what now? You going to look for a publisher?"

"No. That story will never see the light of day. I'm going to spend the next month or so polishing it. I may even hire a grad student to help me edit it. Then, I'll use it as part of my applications. When I get my MFA? That's when I'll write my bestseller."

I sipped my beer with a sigh. "It must be nice to have your whole life mapped out. I'm going to end up flipping burgers."

"DINNER'S READY."

Jeff's voice brought me back to the present. He was sitting across from me. When I turned my attention to him, he gestured to the casserole dishes he had placed in the center of the table.

"Help yourself."

I spooned a little of each dish onto my plate. As he did the same, I took a bite. "This is amazing."

"Thanks. My last roommate, before I got my own place? He was a chef, and he taught me how to cook more than ramen."

I shook my head. "There is no other food." As he laughed, I glanced around. "So, I thought you taught at your old high school."

Jeff raised his eyebrows. "You stalking me?"

I rolled my eyes. "Your sister is my best friend. She's told me all about you. So, why are you here and not in Kensington?"

Jeff's expression turned somber. "After Lisa ... I figured I'd spend the summer here, sorting through everything so I can sell the place."

I gasped. "You can't! It's been in your family for, like, three generations."

"Everywhere I look, I see my family. Did Lisa tell you? When Mom died, we found all Dad's clothes were still in the attic. He'd been gone for, what, ten years at that point? And Mom still had all his things. I had just finished going through it all when Lisa passed. So now, I have to do it all over again. I'll do it because it has to get done. But then, I'm walking away."

There was a mixture of anger and pain in both Jeff's words and his expression. He looked like he wanted to cry and throw something at the same time. My heart broke for him. I might not have had the best relationship with my family, but at least they were still there when I needed them. Jeff had no one. I wanted to wrap my arms around him and tell him everything would be okay.

"I'll help you." At Jeff's confused look, I shrugged. "Going through Lisa's things. I'll help. If you want."

Jeff nodded slowly, taking a long sip from his mug before responding. "I'd like that."

I sent him a cautious smile. "Me, too."

WHEN WE FINISHED EATING, I HELPED JEFF WITH the dishes, and he gave me the five-cent tour. After pointing out a dining room with dark furniture that matched the wood paneling, he led me into a cozy den. I glanced at the orange shag carpet and garish couches—bright yellow with a flower print. I doubted I was older than anything in this room.

Frowning at Jeff, I shook my head. "You realize you're never going to be able to sell this, right? It's too dated. I mean, the kitchen was okay. At least you have newer appliances, but this?"

Jeff scowled. "I don't care about the money. I just want to be rid of this place."

He stalked out of the room. I caught up with him at the top of the stairs. Like the rest of the house, they were carpeted in an ugly beige that looked so dirty and worn, it was oddly comforting.

Three doors stood at the top of the stairs. Jeff pointed to the closed one on the left. "That's my parents' room. All

Lisa's things from her apartment? They're in there. You can pick through it in the morning." He gestured to the closed door on the right. "You can sleep in her room. If you need anything, I'm over here." He pointed to the only open door before stalking inside and slamming it.

With a sigh, I put my hand on the knob of my friend's room and slowly turned. A thousand images flashed through my mind, all different variations of Lisa's college dorm. None of them matched the room I saw as I crossed the threshold.

The plush carpet was the color a pristine beach sand, a perfect complement to walls as blue as the sky on a cloudless day. The cover on the twin bed faded from white at the top to navy at the bottom, with realistic dolphins swimming through the middle. On the walls were some framed posters and hand-drawn pictures, all of sea creatures. A barren white desk held a lighthouse-shaped lamp, while a shell-encrusted one sat on the matching nightstand. The only thing missing was the sound of crashing waves. This room felt like Lisa.

I crossed to the desk, but I wasn't sure what I would find. The only thing on the surface was a blotter, the calendar dated two years ago. Opening the top drawer, I found the usual detritus of broken writing implements, correction fluid, and empty index cards. The one beside it held an assortment of hard floppy discs and a few data CDs, all blank.

Feeling fatigued, I brought my bag to the bed. Though it wasn't that late, the emotional toil of the day was catching up with me. I could use a nice relaxing soak in the tub.

Frowning, I made a slow circle. Jeff hadn't shown me the bathroom. I had seen one downstairs, but that didn't have a shower. Where was the real one?

There were several doors in the room. The one near the bed proved to be a closet, but the one on the opposite side was the bathroom.

After Lisa's pristine room, I was a little surprised by the cluttered counter. An electric razor lay next to a pintail comb. A bottle of contact solution sat beside thin wire-rimmed glasses. I glimpsed behind the shower curtain. There was shampoo and a bar of soap.

If I were going to soak in the tub, I would need bubbles. Or at least salts. There had to be some somewhere. Lisa had loved baths even more than I did.

I checked the cabinet under the sink, but that was full of cleaning supplies. Frowning, I glanced at the other two doors in the room. Why on earth did the bathroom have two linen closets?

I opened the one beside the tub, finding towels in addition to the bath salts and bubbles. After pulling out what I would need, curiosity got the better of me and I peeked into the other closet.

Except it wasn't a closet. Sitting in the corner of the room, on a sea of plush black carpet, was a bed nearly identical to Lisa's. Instead of a dolphin spread, it had a dark gray duvet. Jeff sat upon it in his underwear. Until he saw me.

Swearing, he jumped to his feet, grabbing a pillow to cover his tighty-whities. "What are you doing?"

"I'm . . . I'm sorry." Though I knew I should turn away, my eyes were glued to Jeff's chest. Well-defined and covered with only a thin layer of hair. I might have forgotten how to blink.

"Did you need something?"

Jeff's voice brought my eyes back to his face. I shook my head, mostly to clear it. "Uh, no. I mean, I was going to take a bath and, uh, I was looking for a towel."

He frowned, using the hand not holding the pillow to point behind me. "They're in the bathroom closet."

I nodded. "Oh, great. I'll just . . ." I pointed over my shoulder as I stepped backward. Jeff watched me with narrow eyes until I closed the bathroom door.

When I finally sunk into the bath, I shut my eyes, letting the stress of my day seep from my pores. My mind drifted to Jeff. He was right. I knew so much about him that he felt like family. Maybe some sort of distant cousin.

Yet, he had been so different from my mental image of him. I wasn't sure what I had expected, but I was realizing I knew nothing about him.

And I wanted to.

Stacey couldn't believe how many students died each year. They couldn't all have overdosed, could they? According to the police blotter in the newspaper archives, they had. She had found over forty names in the last decade, more than half of them female.

How far back should she go for her research paper? At first, she was planning to focus on the past few years. But her gut was telling her this was a sign of some sort of epidemic.

Stacey wanted to know when this overdose trend started. Drugs became popular during the sixties, right? She would look back at least that far.

With a sigh, she returned to the microfilm machine. She had another hour until the library closed. How many more names would she add to her list in that time?

Chapter 3

WEDNESDAY MORNING, I WOKE UP DISORIENTED.
It took me a moment to remember where I was. When I
did, I rolled onto my back, closing my eyes with a sigh.

What was I doing here? I had come to Maine to visit
Lisa. And spent the night at the house of a guy I hardly
knew. He could be an ax murderer. What if he killed his
parents and sister, and I was next?

I rolled over with a sigh, watching the rays of sunlight
streaming through the window play with the dust motes
floating around them. I was being ridiculous. Lisa's father
had died in a boating accident ages ago. Her mother had
suffered a long battle with breast cancer. My best friend
had slipped off the rocks.

I frowned. How was that even possible? Lisa was
always at that lighthouse. She had witnessed great
storms off the shore. She knew when it was safe to be on
the jetty. How could she have lost her footing?

I sat upright. Why had she even been there? Wasn't
school still in session? Didn't she stay on campus except
for a week or two over the summer? Why on earth had she
been at that lighthouse?

I flopped back against my pillow with a sigh. Why
couldn't Lisa be the sort of person to have a diary?
Despite all her attempts when we were younger, she was
always more focused on her stories than on documenting
her day. Maybe if she had, then I would have understood
how she had died.

I wasn't sure why it mattered, but as I climbed out of
bed, I realized I wasn't going to find closure until I knew

how Lisa had died. Not the part about falling off the rocks. I had to understand what she was doing there in the first place.

Maybe I would find some answers in her things. But before I could, I wanted to earn my keep. Dressing quickly, I headed downstairs to make breakfast.

And bumped into the open refrigerator door. I stepped backward, rubbing my nose with a frown.

"Ow."

"You okay?"

If I hadn't known Jeff's voice, I probably would not have recognized the man peering around the door. His disheveled hair and bare chest suggested he had not been out of bed much longer than I had. The well-defined abs and wire glasses made me have thoughts on how I could get him back there.

He took a step closer, concern written on his face. "Katie? You okay?"

Oh. Right. He had asked a question. I gave a slow nod. "Yeah. Fine. I wasn't watching where I was going."

Not looking wholly convinced, he gestured to the fridge. "Can I get you something?"

I bit my lip. "Oh. I, uh, was going to offer that to you. You know. Since you let me stay here last night."

An amused expression passed over his face. Did he not think I could make breakfast? Sure, I wasn't about to win any culinary contests. But I knew how to scramble an egg.

Before I could defend myself, Jeff gestured to the coffeemaker. "I'm good with coffee. But feel free to help yourself."

As he poured himself a mug, I glanced in the fridge. Not only was it stocked, but most of the food looked fresh. Fruits and vegetables were in little mesh bags. Brown paper wrapped what I could only assume was meat, possibly fish. The milk was in glass bottles. I could feel my jaw drop, the cold air numbing my tongue.

I must have been ogling too long, because I was still staring, mouth agape, when Jeff started breathing over my shoulder. "Everything okay? Need help finding something?"

I spun around, nearly bumping my nose again, this time on his bare shoulder. As he took a step back, I pointed behind me.

"I have never seen that much food. And you live alone."

He sent me a sheepish smile. "I may have gone a little overboard at the Farmer's Market yesterday. But I enjoy supporting our local farmers. Find what you're looking for?"

I frowned. "I don't remember what I even wanted. Eggs, I guess. Maybe an onion?"

Jeff reached around me to pull ingredients from the refrigerator, his bare chest inches from my nose. As he placed a carton of eggs on the counter, he glanced at me with raised eyebrows. "You sure you're okay?"

I nodded. "Yeah. Fine. Uh, I need a pan."

Shaking his head, Jeff pointed to the pans hanging above the kitchen sink. Feeling my cheeks warm, I grabbed the frying pan. I was about an inch too short to make the handle slide off the hook. I stood on my toes and managed to free the pan. Unfortunately, the hook came with it. As I returned to the ground, the hook bounced off the top of my head. Jeff almost spit his coffee across the room.

Glaring at him, I set the pan on the stove and grabbed a knife from the block. The cutting board was already on the counter, so I turned my back on my host and chopped a small piece off the onion, dicing it before returning the rest to the refrigerator. While I was there, I grabbed the butter.

When the pat hit the skillet, its sizzle told me the pan was ready. I dropped the onions into the melted butter and scanned the counter. A canister in the corner held a flat wooden spatula. Using it, I tossed the onions for a moment while they browned, then scattered them around the pan and grabbed an egg. With one hand, I banged it against the edge of the pan. Moving it to the center, I placed my thumb in the crack and split it apart, allowing the egg to drip over my onions. After tossing the shell into the sink, I repeated this with another egg. Quickly rinsing my hands, I grabbed the spatula, piercing the yolk and scrambling the eggs around the pan.

I could feel Jeff breathing in my ear as he glanced over my shoulder. "Did you just crack those eggs with one hand?"

I nodded. "When I was a kid, my mother used to get so mad at me for doing it. But I almost never get any shells."

He shook his head in awe, pointing to the cabinet beneath the sink. "The garbage is under there."

I flipped my eggs before tossing the shells in the trash and again washing my hands. When Jeff placed a plate on the cutting board, I smiled. "Thanks."

He pointed above his head. "I'm going to, uh, shower and stuff. You good?"

I nodded. "Yeah. Thanks."

"Holler if you need anything."

After watching Jeff carry his mug from the room, I turned off the stove, scraping my eggs onto my plate. Pouring myself half a mug of coffee, I took my breakfast to the table, taking my first bite with my eyes closed. Not bad. The perfect comfort food to face the day ahead.

AFTER WASHING MY PLATE AND THE SKILLET, I topped off my coffee and headed upstairs to the master bedroom. I turned the knob slowly, uncertain what I would find on the other side. Part of me expected it to be like my parents' room, dark furniture with leopard print bedding and matching curtains. Part of me thought it would be identical to the room where I slept last night.

However, it was neither. The powder blue bedspread complimented the oak furniture and matched the ruffled pillows near the headboard. The sun trickling in through pale sheers cast everything in a blue light.

Stacked in neat piles around the room were the white file storage boxes my mother loved to use. The sturdy cardboard containers each had a removable lid and cut-outs to use as handles. None were labeled. I lifted the lid on the one closest to me. Clothes.

The room felt stuffy, as if no one had been in here in months. I had a feeling no one had. I drew the curtains and opened the window, taking a deep breath of the salty air before turning back to the room. With a sigh, I hefted the box onto the bed and removed the lid.

Whoever had packed it had done a poor job. Clothes had been tossed inside haphazardly, probably smushed down to fit as many as possible. Nothing was folded. Granted, I tended to pack my suitcases like this, but neat-as-a-pin Lisa would cringe if she ever saw the disarray.

Since it was already a mess, I dumped the box on the bed and held up the first item. A pretty pink sundress Lisa had worn on our annual trip to the Cape. I folded it neatly and returned it to the box. Jeff could probably sell it at a consignment shop.

I picked up a pair of jeans. They were tattered and worn, but not in a stylish way. After checking the pockets, I folded them and placed them on the overturned lid. It wasn't worth trying to sell these. They could go straight to charity. Maybe someone could repurpose them as a purse or something.

After sorting all the clothes in the box, I removed the lid of another. This one held desk supplies, but I could go through those later. For now, I was in a mood to sort clothes. After grabbing some writing utensils, I labeled the box in pencil and moved it to the floor.

The box beneath it held socks and undergarments. I dumped the contents onto the bed, only to return the items one by one. When I added the rest of the clothes for the donation pile, the box was full. I wrote "donate" on the side with a marker before moving the box to the space beside the door.

I spent my morning sorting, separating clothes into piles while labeling and rearranging the remaining boxes by type. By the time my stomach declared it was ready for a break, I had created three boxes of consignment clothes and two for donation. I had even sorted through Lisa's bedding and towels, placing them in separate boxes, since I wasn't sure what Jeff intended to do with them.

I exited the room with a sigh. When I had volunteered to sort through Lisa's things, I had thought I would be *helping* Jeff, not doing the task alone. But I hadn't seen him since breakfast.

As I entered the kitchen, I found him preparing a salad. He smiled, pointing at me with a large knife.

"Hey. I was just about to come find you. I was going to make salad and sandwiches for lunch."

I shrugged. "Sounds good."

He nodded, looking as if he wanted to say more. His mouth opened, but he shut it without uttering a sound, turning his attention back to the head of lettuce in front of him.

I glanced around. "How can I help?"

Jeff didn't look up. "Just have a seat. Take a break. I've got this."

After grabbing a glass of water from the pitcher in the fridge, I plopped into a kitchen chair. It was the first time I had sat since breakfast. I hadn't realized how much my feet were protesting until I propped them on the neighboring chair.

I was also thirstier than I had thought. As soon as I put up my feet, I drained my glass. I stared at it with a sigh. I didn't feel like getting up again. But I really wanted more water.

I was still contemplating my predicament when Jeff brought the salad to the table. He nodded to the empty glass. "Want more water?"

I shook my head. "Nah. I can get it. I was just resting a minute."

He waved a dismissive hand. "No biggie." He grabbed the pitcher from the fridge, placing it on the table beside the salad bowl before returning to the counter.

I smiled. "Thanks."

He again opened his mouth like he wanted to say

more, but seemed to decide against it. While I refilled my glass, he brought bread and lunch meat to the table, along with some condiments and a bottle of Italian dressing. He gestured to the spread as he sat across from me.

"Help yourself."

I grabbed a couple of slices of bread, lathered mayonnaise on them, and made a turkey sandwich with lettuce and cheese. Across from me, Jeff had opted for salad. The silence between us rapidly turned uncomfortable. I took a long drink of my water before looking across the table. "So—"

"How's—"

The silence must have gotten to Jeff as well. We both gave nervous laughs, and he indicated I should go first.

"I was just going to say that I sorted through all of Lisa's clothes. I made two piles: one for donation and one you can bring to a consignment shop."

"Thanks. That's really a big help. So, what are your plans for this afternoon? Did you want a tour of the area?"

I raised my eyebrows. "I drove through the downtown area last night. Even saw the lighthouse where—well, I saw the lighthouse."

Jeff's face fell. "Huh. Sounds like you saw the whole town. Well, how about this? Let's put a couple more hours into sorting through the boxes and I'll take you to the co-op for dinner."

Since I had no idea what he meant, I gave a noncommittal shrug and got to my feet. "I'm going to go tackle the desk supplies. There are a bunch of floppies. Was that Lisa's computer I saw in the spare room?"

Jeff nodded. "Yeah. I can set that up in your room, if you want."

"That would be great. Thanks."

I placed my plate in the sink, but Jeff was helping himself to seconds, so I left everything on the table for him to put away and headed upstairs.

Stacey stared at the graph she had made. It was almost shaped like the letter N. There was a sharp spike in the mid-sixties, which had plummeted before the end of the decade. But over the past nine or ten years, the number of overdoses had risen again. Almost linearly.

Stacey let her eyes wander as she contemplated this. Was it some new drug? Was there a change in school policy? Was this trend mirrored in other universities in the area?

Stacey felt a flutter of excitement. This was it! She had found her research project. She would figure out why so many people were dying. And she wouldn't stop until she found some answers.

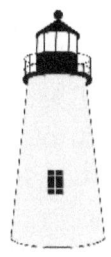

Chapter 4

I SPENT MY AFTERNOON SORTING THROUGH THE various knickknacks Lisa had accumulated in her apartment. I knew her small collection of stuffed animals had held sentimental value. Most were gifts from ex-boyfriends. But she was gone, and I was not attached to any of them. I placed them all in a box for the donation pile. If Jeff wanted, he could always keep them.

I collected nearly an entire box of scented candles, incense, and their paraphernalia. I brought them into Lisa's bedroom, arranging them decoratively on the dresser, filling the top drawer with whatever didn't fit.

I brought the toiletries into the shared bathroom, finding homes for everything in the linen closet. I figured if Jeff were desperate enough, he may elect to use Lisa's cucumber body wash over his mountain fresh bar soap.

While I worked, Jeff wandered in and out of the master bedroom a few times to retrieve the components of Lisa's computer, eventually lingering in her room to assemble it. I emerged from the bathroom to find him squatting behind the desk. I was going to leave him be. But as I passed, he banged on the keyboard, uttering some choice words.

I bit back a smirk. "Not working?"

"No, it's working." He pushed the keyboard away vehemently as he got to his feet. "I just don't know her passwords."

I shrugged. "No biggie. I'll play with it tonight. I'm sure I can figure it out. If not, I'll just log in as a guest. It looks like she saved everything on these floppies, anyway."

Jeff sighed, glancing at his watch. "I know it's early, but you in the mood for dinner?"

No, because it was still too early for the early bird special. But I didn't want to be rude. I gestured over my shoulder. "I kind of wanted to see how far I could get in there."

Jeff nodded. "Yeah. That's probably a good idea."

He led the way back to the spare room, stopping so suddenly just over the threshold that I nearly bumped into him. Since he was slowly turning his head around the room, I assumed he was surveying my progress.

I squeezed past him, crossing to the stack of boxes beside the bed. "This is all stuff for you to take to the consignment shop." I gestured to another stack. "That's donation." I pointed to the foot of the bed. "These boxes are linens. I wasn't sure if you wanted to keep them or donate them."

Jeff shook his head slowly. "Wow. I never expected you to get through all this. Was there anything you—you know. Wanted to keep?"

Biting my lip, I pointed to the boxes I had yet to sort. "That's Lisa's writing. Well, at least some of it is. I was kind of hoping I could take her stories."

Jeff nodded. "I think she would love that."

There was a catch in his voice. I couldn't blame him. I was close to tears myself. Wordlessly, I grabbed a box and brought it to the bed. It was the one I had labeled *desk supplies* hours ago. I inclined my head to the door to indicate Jeff should follow me as I went back to Lisa's room.

I had planned to dump the box on the bed, but I didn't want to ruin her pretty comforter. Setting the box on the floor, I ran to the bathroom, pulling a dark bath towel from the closet. I spread this over the bed before emptying the contents of the box on it.

Jeff gave a small laugh. "Lisa would freak if she saw you do that."

"I know, right? I always envied how anal she was. Me? I need to see the mess and sort through it like this."

"So, what do we do with all this?"

I found a small memo pad, opening it to a random blank page before passing it to Jeff. "You can go through all the pens and see what to keep and what to toss."

BY THE TIME MY STOMACH STARTED RUMBLING, we had emptied the last box. For better or worse, we had gone through all of Lisa's things. Beside her bed was a box of notebooks—her stories that I would read when I got home.

Since I had spent all day sorting through boxes, I needed a quick shower before going out to dinner. After throwing on a sundress, I found Jeff in the kitchen.

He had freshened up as well, changing into clean jeans and a T-shirt. His blue ball cap had a large red letter B. I smirked as I nodded. "Go Red Sox."

His eyes lit up as he held open the back door. "Hey. They have a shot at the pennant this year."

I just shook my head. I wasn't a big baseball fan, and even I knew the Red Sox hadn't made it to the World Series since they lost Babe Ruth. But I was from the land of Red Sox versus Yankees. I had learned at an early age that baseball was a more debatable subject over the dinner table than politics or religion.

Climbing into Jeff's truck, I decided to change the subject. "So, what is this co-op you keep mentioning? Because, every time you say it, I get flashbacks of three-year-olds."

Jeff raised his eyebrows, sparing me a quick glance as he pulled out of the driveway. "Come again?"

I shrugged. "When I was little, the neighborhood moms had this group they called the Baker Street Co-Op. All the kids too little for school would come to my house so their moms could go to the grocery store or doctor or whatever.

They'd play with my toys, we'd have lunch, then we'd all lay on blankets in the living room while my mom read us a story. After our nap, we'd play outside till their moms came back. The next day, we'd go to someone else's house and do the same thing."

Jeff gave a small laugh. "Cute. And this place isn't anything like that."

Not that he gave me any clues about what it *was* like. Then again, he didn't really need to. A short time later, he pulled into a driveway. A small wooden sign, no bigger than a mailbox, read Copper Cove Fishermen's Co-op. The gravel drive was lined with the wire cages I had seen everywhere since coming into town. I pointed to a stack as Jeff parked in the grass.

"What are those things?"

"Traps. Those round ones there are for crabs." I looked at where he was pointing. The bright yellow rectangle had a domed top and was divided into three rooms. Beside it was one that was more rectangular. Jeff gestured to it. "Those are for lobsters."

As we climbed out of the car, the smell of salt air and fish tickled my nose. Jeff motioned to the end of the driveway. Past the trees, I could see a dock where men were pulling similar cages off a boat.

"This is the co-op. Fishermen bring their catches here. A lot of them store the cages they're not using."

"So, we're going to buy fish from them for dinner?"

Jeff laughed and pointed to a blue shed to our right. It was in a vast field and had a wooden swing set beside it. A white sign hung from the roof: *Copper Cove Fishermen's Co-op.*

I gave a knowing nod. "Oh. I get it. We're going to buy them from the store."

Shaking his head, Jeff led the way to the back of the building. It was bigger than I had realized, maybe the size of my apartment. Large windows looked inside, where I could see a dozen tables with chairs. A counter in the back separated a kitchen from the dining room. Beside it, a huge chalkboard listed today's menu.

Jeff held open a screen door, gesturing for me to enter ahead of him. I read the menu as I did, surprised at the prices. I was no expert, but I was pretty sure a steamed lobster went for twice as much at the restaurants back home.

Biting my lip, I sent Jeff a skeptical look. "Uh, is there a reason the prices are so low? I mean, they're good quality, right? I'm not going to get food poisoning?"

Jeff laughed, the sound mixing with the noise from the kitchen. "You can't get any fresher. They caught these fish today."

I was still hesitant, but how could I turn down a fresh Maine lobster? When was the last time I had even had one? I couldn't remember.

I glanced around the restaurant. We were the only patrons. A bored woman about my age was doodling on an order pad behind the register. When I approached her, she smiled.

"Welcome to the Copper Cove Co-op. What can I get for you?"

"I'll have the steamed lobster."

She nodded. "Single or double?"

"Oh, man. Single. That's more than enough."

She gave a small laugh. "And did you want the combo meal?"

"Uh, what's that?" I was picturing fries and a soda, but I had a feeling it meant something different here.

"Comes with coleslaw, homemade chips, and a dinner roll."

I nodded. "Sounds good to me."

"Anything else? Drink?"

I shook my head. Jeff had packed us a couple of beers, claiming the co-op was BYOB. I had never heard of such a thing—at least, not at a restaurant—so I figured it was best not to mention it. The girl rang up my order, and I handed her a twenty. I tossed a couple of dollars of my change into the tip jar before pocketing the rest.

After Jeff ordered his meal, he nodded his head to the door. "Come here. I want to show you something."

I followed him back outside. On the side of the building was a small screen room. Inside, a woman reached into a large tank and removed a lobster. I watched as she tied a string around it and dropped it into—

I spun around to look at Jeff. "Is that a hot tub?"

He nodded, his smile bright. "Pretty much."

Growing up, a friend of mine had a hot tub on her back porch. It could fit half a dozen of us fairly comfortably. This wasn't that kind of tub. It looked more like the one I saw that one time I went into the sports trainer's room in college. It was almost as tall as me and about the size of a Hula-Hoop.

The woman lifted a string hanging off the side, tugging until a large mesh bag emerged. I gestured to it with my head.

"What's in there?"

"Steamers. Sometimes, it's an assortment of clams, oysters, scallops. Sometimes it's just clams."

I watched in mesmerized silence, not bothered by the seafood smell that usually made me nauseous, until the woman pulled two lobsters from the pot. They had entered the bath the color of dull bricks, but now they were bright, shiny fire engines. The woman untied the string and removed the rubber bands around the claws before disappearing into the kitchen.

Jeff placed a hand on my shoulder. "That's probably us."

Nodding, I turned to go back into the restaurant. I was almost at the door when I heard the cashier call our order numbers.

"Twenty-four! Twenty-five!"

I grabbed my cafeteria tray, overburdened with my meal, and waited for Jeff to lead the way. He opted for an outside picnic table. Once settled, he reached into the little cooler and removed two beers. After opening both, he passed me the better one and inclined his toward mine.

We clicked necks, and he smiled. "Thank you. For going thorough all those boxes for me. I was going to help you, but every time I tried . . ."

I nodded, hearing his voice falter. I wanted to comfort him, reach over and give him a hug, but did I really know him well enough to do so?

He took a long drink from his bottle before busying himself with his lobster. I did the same. I pulled meat from the tail, tossing it into the bowl of melted butter on my tray. After emptying the meat from the claws, I twisted off the knuckles and used the lobster pick to poke out the meat. I tore off each leg, sucking out the meat and tossing it into the butter.

While the lobster marinated, I peeled the shell from the body and scraped the ribs, careful to avoid the tomalley. When I finished picking clean my lobster, I set aside the carcass, glancing at Jeff as I pulled my butter bowl toward me.

He had dissected his lobster much as I had and was eating the marinated meat. The silence between us grew uncomfortable.

I bit my lip, trying to think of something to say. Figuring the weather was better than nothing, I gestured toward the dock. "So—"

"What—"

Giggling, I pointed to Jeff with my fork. "Go ahead. Your turn."

His face was red. "Well, it's just, I read that letter you sent my sister last week. Why are you working at a coffee shop? I thought Lisa said you wanted to be a doctor."

I gave a weak laugh. "Yeah. That didn't work out so well. Still trying to figure out what I wanna be when I grow up."

Jeff smiled. "I know the feeling. I always thought I would end up as a museum curator."

"How'd you end up teaching?"

He shrugged. "Kept in touch with my favorite teacher. She told me about the job opening. Said I should apply. So, I did."

I raised my eyebrows. "They hired you? Just like that? Even though you didn't have a teaching degree?"

He nodded. "Yup. It's complicated, but I was able to apply for emergency certification because they had literally no other applicants. Not many people want to teach in the consolidated systems. They'd rather go to Portland or Augusta."

"So, do you still have dreams of becoming a curator?"

He shrugged. "Nah. I'm part of the historical society, both here and in Kensington. I find that fulfilling enough. Turns out I really enjoy teaching."

I poked at my dinner. "That moment when a kid's face lights up when they suddenly understand something they've been struggling with."

Jeff smirked. "Sounds like you speak from experience."

I shrugged. "I tutor a couple of elementary school kids in math and science. Been doing it since high school. Took on a few SAT prep students last year."

"Well, if the coffee shop thing doesn't work out, science teachers are always in high demand. You can probably get a job for next year. Just saying."

I pushed away my plate. I hadn't come here for career advice from a virtual stranger. It was time to change the subject. "So, there's something that's been bugging me. Why wasn't Lisa at school?"

Jeff raised his eyebrows, clearly thrown by the change in conversation. "Huh?"

I frowned. "When she ... That night. Why was she here in Copper Cove? Why wasn't she at school?"

Jeff stared into the water. "We talked every week. Just to check up on each other. The last time she called, she sounded nervous. Anxious."

He turned back to me with a sigh, and I could see tears in the corner of his eyes. "I thought it was just the pressure of writing her book. And, honestly, I was annoyed. She called while I was getting ready for a date, and I didn't want to listen to her whine about her stupid book. I cut her off without really listening to her. That was the last time I spoke to her."

I bit my lip. "I've been thinking about something all day. Lisa loved to go out on the jetty. It was her favorite thinking place."

Jeff nodded. "She used to ride her bike down there when we were kids."

"Exactly. She, of all people, should have known if it wasn't safe to be out there."

Jeff took a sip of beer, speaking slowly after he swallowed. "You think maybe she went out there when it wasn't safe on purpose?"

I studied him for a moment. There was something about his posture, his pursed lips. "You've already had that thought."

He nodded. "She was so distraught. I think she was trying to tell me something, and I blew her off. You asked why she wasn't at school? I think something happened, and she came home for solace. She went out to the rocks to get peace. And when I shut her out—"

When Jeff's voice cracked, I rushed to the opposite side of the bench, taking him into my arms. As he sobbed on my shoulder, I rubbed his back, tears stinging my own eyes. "You're not responsible. Whatever happened, you didn't force her onto those rocks." I pushed him away gently so I could look into his eyes. "You know how you can make things right? Help me read through her writing journals. Maybe she put enough of herself into one of her stories that we could figure out what happened."

Jeff nodded with a sniff. "Okay. Let's do that." He glanced at the table. "Now a good time to start?"

I smiled. "Let's blow this place."

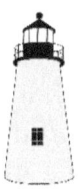

WHILE I HAD BEEN SORTING THROUGH LISA'S desk supplies, I had stumbled across an index card full of random phrases. I had a feeling one of those would get me into her computer. As Jeff settled himself on the bed with one of Lisa's journals, I sat at the desk and entered the first one.

Bingo. I smirked at Jeff. "I'm in."

He narrowed his eyes at me. "No way." When I angled the monitor so he could see, he swore. "That's just not fair."

I rolled my eyes. "Your anal sister wrote out all her passwords. I just took a guess that the top one was to get into her computer."

"What was it?"

"*password.* All lowercase."

Jeff just shook his head. "That's a dumb password."

I said nothing. It was the same one I used on my own computer.

I busied myself flipping through Lisa's floppies, which were neatly organized in a caddy. According to their labels, she had a disk for each semester of college, all containing class notes and papers. Another one held all her transcripts, probably from when she was applying to graduate schools. After a divider were her various stories. She liked to place each one on a different disk, since she saved nearly every draft.

I smiled when I found her senior project, popping the floppy into the machine. There were two folders: *research* and *drafts.* I clicked on the latter, discovering another set of folders: *old stuff* and *final project.* After a little more searching, I found the paper she had submitted to her advisor. The one that had helped her acceptance into the master's degree program.

I glanced through the first few pages, but I had already read this story. With a sigh, I ejected the disk and continued my search. If I wanted to figure out why Lisa died, I would need something more recent.

Unfortunately, her stories were in alphabetical order with random working titles. I had no idea which one was the most recent. As organized as Lisa was, she didn't seem to date her disks. Except for the class notes. With a sigh, I flipped back to the first one in the caddy and inserted it into the machine.

Lisa's graduate seminars had been structured differently than our undergraduate classes had been. She had attended workshops during the summer and winter semesters, while spending the fall and spring ones working on her novel. I tried to read her notes, but I couldn't comprehend most of it. Why did she take a seminar on world building? She wrote contemporary fiction, not fantasy.

"Ugh!" I banged my head on the desk, probably a little harder than I meant to.

Jeff looked up from the bed. "Everything okay?"

I gestured to the monitor. "No. It's all Sanskrit to me."

He raised his eyebrows. "I think the phrase is *It's all Greek to me.*"

I rolled my eyes. "Greek I could understand. Well, at least Ancient Greek. But this? Way over my head."

I saw a mixture of expressions cross Jeff's face before he slid to the edge of the bed. "Why don't you take a break? Go through these journals with me."

With a shrug, I sat beside him. "Find anything interesting?"

"Not really. Mostly rough drafts, full of cross-outs and notes in the margins. But I think I'm reading some of her earlier stuff. Every heroine is named Stacey."

I gave a small laugh. "That was one of my favorite things about Lisa. She was so in love with the name, she used it for every story. It wasn't until she finished the draft that she would change the character's name. She said she needed to get to the end of a story to know her character well enough to name her."

Jeff sent me a look of disbelief. "That's ridiculous."

I shrugged. "I thought so, too, but it seemed to work for her. Pass me a journal."

Stacey looked at the two lists she had made. The one on her right contained the names of twenty people who had overdosed over the past forty years. It was a lot shorter than she had expected it to be. There was a mixture of men and women. The youngest was a teenager, and the oldest had retired a few months before his death. She couldn't find any connection between any of them.

She turned to her other list. Twenty women. The youngest was eighteen, while the oldest was thirty. All had died within the last fifteen years. Each of them had a connection to Seacliff University. Most had been students at the time of their death.

What was it about the school that had resulted in all these deaths? There had to be another connection. And Stacey was determined to find it.

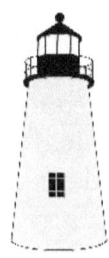

Chapter 5

THE FIRST THING I NOTICED WHEN I WOKE Thursday morning was that I was not alone. I was facing the wall with an arm slung over my waist.

I stiffened slightly. Although I had dated a few guys, I had never had a sleepover. I wasn't exactly sure what I was supposed to do.

Of course, this wasn't even that kind of sleepover. So why was I so uncomfortable? It wasn't like anything had happened between me and Jeff. We had been reading and must have fallen asleep.

He stirred, tightening the arm around my waist and coming closer. I was torn. Part of me wanted to run away, but part of me didn't want to move. Waking up in someone else's arms was kind of nice.

I closed my eyes and attempted to relax. But the harder I tried, the more I obsessed about the situation. I needed to focus on something else.

I tried to remember the stories I had read last night. Most of them I had recognized. Lisa had been sending me final drafts since high school. But there had been three that were new to me.

The first was a short story about a girl trying to work up the courage to ask out her crush. It had sounded like a middle school drama and I was pretty sure Lisa had written it when we were kids.

The protagonist in the second one was about the same age, but it wasn't a romance. This Stacey was trying to locate her birth parents. It felt very much like some movies I had watched in high school and Lisa had filled the margins with notes questioning how realistic the situation was.

Neither of those stories had felt recent. But the last one had. Written on looseleaf and stored in a binder, Stacey was a college student trying to do a research project when she noticed many people at the school had been dying. Some sort of drug pandemic was leading to a lot of accidental deaths. Even though I hadn't read very far before falling asleep, I had noticed a lot of scribbling in the margins. Could Lisa have discovered a similar situation?

There had to be more to her story. Knowing my friend, she would have kept a notebook of research and ideas. Maybe a file folder or another binder. Though she liked computer backups, she always wrote everything down. So where was it?

My bladder decided that, no matter how nice it felt to be in Jeff's arms, I needed to get out of bed. After visiting the bathroom, I grabbed Lisa's story and made my way to the computer.

In the front cover of the binder was a sticky note with a list of numbers under a heading of *Middleton Mirror*. I had no clue what that was, so I asked Jeeves. The search engine pulled up a bunch of newspapers from around the country. How on earth was I going to narrow it down?

I considered the story. The deaths had been at the main character's college. Could Lisa have based it on her own school?

Probably not. She had attended Down East University. I surfed the school website before finding their paper. It was called the *Gull Gazette*. And the college was in Southbridge, Maine. No mention of Middleton anywhere.

I glanced at the note again. The first number was 8-29-2. Was that a date? Frowning, I went back to my initial search results and clicked on each newspaper, combing the archives to find articles from August 29th of last year. But none of the papers mentioned a student dying at a local college.

"Mmm. Morning."

I turned to the groggy voice behind me. Jeff was smiling at me from the bed. His hair was mussed, and he had marks on his face from sleeping with his glasses on.

He sat upright with a yawn. "Whatcha doing?"

I shrugged. "Trying to find a newspaper. You ever hear of the *Middleton Mirror?*"

Jeff nodded, scooting to the end of the bed. "Yeah, of course. It's the local paper."

I frowned. "But this is Copper Cove."

"Well, yeah. Middleton is the name of the county."

I asked Jeeves to find me the *Middleton Mirror* in Maine and clicked on the first search result. As soon as the page opened, I kicked myself for not recognizing the name. This was where I had read Lisa's obituary and the story about her death.

I again searched the archives for articles from August 29th. Within minutes, I was staring at the picture of a woman about my age who had killed herself during the summer session. The story was short, more of an obituary and eulogy than a traditional news article. It wasn't unlike the one about Lisa's death.

As I read, I could feel someone breathing in my ear. I turned, intending to ask Jeff for a little personal space, only to find myself tongue-tied. Standing behind me, he had one hand on the back of my chair while the other was on the desk. He was hunched, his head hovering beside mine as he literally read over my shoulder. He smelled minty-fresh, and I immediately became self-conscious about my own breath. Why hadn't I thought to brush my teeth when I was in the bathroom?

Jeff seemed oblivious to my plight, however. He pointed to the screen as he straightened. "I think I went to high school with her."

I frowned. "Did Lisa know her?"

Jeff shook his head. "Nah. That girl was older than me. Would have graduated before my sister started." He pointed over his shoulder. "I'm gonna make breakfast. Omelets and toast?"

I quickly got to my feet. "I can help."

He shrugged. "I can do it. I *want* to make breakfast."

I bit my lip. "Well, in that case. I'd like to take a quick shower."

"Okay. Great." He gestured to the computer. "We can compare notes while we eat."

AFTER BRUSHING MY TEETH AND TAKING THE quickest shower imaginable, I hurriedly dressed, entering the kitchen as Jeff was sliding an omelet onto a plate. Beside it were two slices of buttered toast. On the table were several small jars of jams and two glasses of orange juice.

I raised my eyebrows as I sat down. "This is a pretty impressive breakfast. I feel like I'm at the diner."

Jeff placed the omelet in front of me with a smile. "I do what I can." Returning to the coffeemaker, he filled two mugs and brought them to the table before grabbing a plate from the oven and sitting across from me. He gestured to my breakfast. "Don't wait for me. Please, eat it while it's hot."

I took a bite, involuntarily closing my eyes to savor it and giving a small moan. When I opened them again, Jeff was smirking at me. As I felt my cheeks grow warm, I quickly took a sip of my juice to hide my embarrassment.

Jeff nodded toward my plate. "Glad you like it."

"It's fantastic. What's in here?"

"Ham, cheese, peppers, onions, mushrooms, fresh spinach. What else? I grounded in some salt and pepper."

"It's incredible."

Jeff shrugged, his face turning slightly scarlet. "It's not that hard. You just throw a bunch of stuff in the skillet and then add an egg. You did it yesterday."

I shook my head. "No, I sauteed an onion. I would have never thought of adding all this stuff. It's great."

Jeff took a long drink of juice, draining half his glass before returning it to the table. "So, did you learn anything last night? About Lisa?"

I sighed. "Maybe? I think I found the story she was writing for her degree."

"Really? Which one?"

"It was in a binder."

Jeff shook his head. "I saw that, but it was all scribbley, so I didn't want to read it. Didn't occur to me that might be her thesis. Or, whatever you want to call it. Did you find anything useful?"

I bit into my toast with a shrug. "Not sure. I only read the first chapter. The main character is trying to find a topic for a research paper. Starts researching newspapers and discovers a drug epidemic at her school. Lots of accidental ODs."

Jeff shoved some eggs into this mouth. "Is that what you were reading this morning?"

"Not quite." I took a quick sip of my coffee. "Lisa had a list of dates from the *Middleton Mirror*. I only looked up the first one. You saw it."

He nodded. "Yeah. But that girl didn't die from drugs."

"No, but she did die. Maybe Lisa used her as inspiration."

Jeff frowned into his coffee mug. "That's pretty morbid."

"Last night, I was reading through the notes she had taken at some seminar or another and she must have written a thousand times: *write what you know*. A lot of caps, underlines, bold, sometimes even highlighted. It seemed to be the theme for her thesis."

Jeff popped the last of his omelet into his mouth before pointing at me with his fork. "You think she was writing about this girl?"

I shrugged. "Maybe not about her, per se, but maybe she was her inspiration. There was a list of dates, and I bet they were all people who had died. I wonder if she knew any of them."

Jeff frowned. "If you find the obituaries, I can look through them. See if any names sound familiar."

When we finished eating, I helped Jeff with the dishes before he followed me upstairs to Lisa's room. While he connected the printer to the computer, I navigated my way through the *Middleton Mirror*. I didn't get very far. Growling in frustration, I tossed the mouse away as I pushed myself from the desk.

Jeff crawled out from behind the computer with raised eyebrows. "Everything okay?"

"No. The stupid online archives only go back one year."

Smirking, he got to his feet. "So?"

"So? How did Lisa even *find* all these dates?"

"Knowing my sister? Probably scanning through microfilm at the library for days at a time."

I frowned. "So, we need to go to her school library?"

Jeff gave a small laugh. "Nah. The town library should have the records we need."

As much as I was hoping to get back to Lisa's story, my gut was telling me we needed to follow her research trail. Grabbing an index card from the desk, I quickly jotted the dates Lisa had listed and turned to Jeff. He was standing in the doorway with a shoebox in his hand.

I sent him a curious look. "What's that?"

Shaking his head, he left the room. "Not important."

Glancing at the shelf, I grabbed some of Lisa's favorite CDs for the ride before following Jeff down the stairs. "Then why do you have it?"

"So many questions. I'll tell you later." He grabbed his keys from a basket near the back door. "Ready?"

No. I wanted to know why he needed to bring a box of sneakers to the library. Judging from the size of the box, they were probably too small for him, anyway. But I let the subject die as I climbed into his truck. He placed the box between us before pulling out of the garage.

As I flipped through the CDs in my hand, Jeff frowned at me. "Whatcha got there?"

I shrugged. "Lisa's music. I thought it would help me feel a little closer to her, you know?"

Jeff groaned. "Please tell me you're not going to torture me with it?"

I smirked. Country wasn't really my favorite genre, either. But I could handle the artists who had made it onto the pop charts.

I opened the Shania case. "What's this?" Frowning, I held up the CD inside. It was homemade. Lisa had labeled it *Stacey's playlist.*

Jeff glanced at me. "Maybe something she listened to when writing?"

I nodded. "Maybe." I popped it in the truck's CD slot, but the stereo wouldn't play.

Jeff shrugged. "She probably formatted it for the computer."

I nodded. "Oh well." I held up the other two CDs in my hand. "Garth or Reba?"

Jeff quickly pressed the button, turning the radio to a local station instead.

When Jeff reached the main road, he turned away from the lighthouse and I recognized some of the surroundings from when I had first driven into Copper Cove. That day, however, I had been so focused on my destination, I hadn't really *seen* anything. Being Jeff's passenger allowed me to pay attention to the sights.

It was even more breathtaking than the last time I had driven this way. Large expanses of rolling farmland. Tall groves of trees. A lot of pine and some maple, but also many I could not identify, despite my biology degree. Along the ground were wildflowers in a rainbow of colors.

After a few minutes, we entered what I had assumed to be the center of Copper Cove. On one side of the road, the river was dammed to create the Copper Cove Swimming Hole. Across the street was a concrete trough with water flowing into it from a metal pipe at the side. A small plaque on the front labeled this as the Copper Cove Spring.

I pointed to it as we passed. "What's that?"

Jeff glanced over his shoulder. "Oh. That's the spring. We can get water there if we lose power to our wells."

"I've never heard of that. It's pretty cool."

Jeff shrugged. "I guess. We've never had to use it. But it's also pretty handy for a quick sip when we're at the swimming hole."

I wasn't sure what else I could say about a public water fountain, so I went back to looking out the window. Several white clapboard buildings, most not much larger than a shack, were clustered together on either side of the road. I read the black-lettered signs above each doorway. Town Office. Fire and Rescue. Post Office. Public Library.

But Jeff didn't pull into the lot. As the surroundings again turned to farmland and trees, I pointed behind me. "Uh, I thought we were going to the library."

He let out a sound somewhere between a snort and a laugh. "That's not a library. That's a shed with a few books. They've got a decent collection, and they have a mahjong club that plays almost every morning. But they won't have what we're looking for. We're going to Belfort."

I wrinkled my nose. "Where's that?"

"You drove through it to get here."

I narrowed my eyes. "How would you know that?"

His exasperated sigh suggested I might have been asking too many questions. But I wasn't about to let the subject drop. I crossed my arms and continued to stare at him.

Jeff completely ignored me. We sat like that for a full five minutes until we reached the beginning of Route 49. I recognized it by the increase in traffic. However, just before the intersection, Jeff pulled into a parking lot behind a cluster of buildings, circling the lot three times before finding a space. Only then did he turn to me.

"Did you, or did you not, come through here on your way into Copper Cove?"

I rolled my eyes. He could have just *told* me this was Belfort instead of sounding all creepy stalkerish. With a sigh, I climbed out of the car.

Stacey's gaze landed on the school newspaper sitting on her desk. Another student had died last week. Someone she knew.

Stacey frowned at the picture. Allie had been in a few of her classes over the years. She was almost a friend.

But that wasn't what was bothering Stacey. If anyone had ever asked, she would have pegged Allie as a high on life kind of girl. Not high for life. How on earth did she OD?

With a sigh, Stacey got to her feet. Allie had lived down the hall. It was time for this investigative reporter to get some answers.

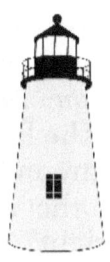

Chapter 6

WE CROSSED THE PARKING LOT, FOLLOWING THE sidewalk to the main intersection. Glancing in both directions, Jeff barely waited for traffic to stop before stepping into the street. Not that it mattered. The cars weren't really going anywhere, anyway. At least we were using a crosswalk. Most of the tourists weren't.

Nestled between a church and a bank was a short walkway to a large brick building set away from the road. We entered a wide two-story rotunda with a card catalog in the center, surrounded by a circle of bookshelves with new releases.

A small glass room on my right held computers and typewriters. To my left was the circulation desk. In the back, the children's department was encased in soundproof windows.

I followed Jeff to a room behind the computers where two microfilm machines sat between windows that looked out into a courtyard. A study table in the center of the room was littered with newspapers, while others hung from a rack beside the door. A shelf sat near the doorway with signs reminding patrons to place the used materials there instead of trying to re-shelve it themselves. Most of the rest of the room contained the large storage cabinets used to store the microfilm.

Jeff headed straight for the nearest one, running his finger along the labels on the drawers. The entire first cabinet held the *Augusta Herald*, dating back over a hundred years. Those papers would be amazing to see.

But we weren't here to research the history of Maine. Jeff and I examined the next few cabinets before finding the one for the *Middleton Mirror*. The top drawer contained all the issues for the last couple of decades.

Biting my lip, I pulled my index card from my pocket. "Might as well start with the most recent editions and work our way backwards, right?"

Jeff nodded. "Works for me."

He pulled two boxes from the top drawer, passing me one as we crossed the room to the machines. Settling into his chair, he sent me a skeptical look. "You *do* know how to use this, right?"

I rolled my eyes. "I wrote a forty-page term paper on the Sacco-Vanzetti trial my junior year of high school. Combed through newspaper articles for nearly a month. Trust me. Me and the microfilm machine? Best buds."

Jeff smirked. "Sacco-Vanzetti, huh? What was your verdict?"

I frowned. "Inconclusive. The trial was definitely unfair, but I never decided if they were innocent or guilty."

"And your teacher let you get away with that?"

I shrugged. "I got the impression he stopped reading halfway through the paper. No one else in my class had written more than ten pages."

"Well, I would have read through the entire thing. And given you a C for your indecision."

I pretended to sneer, but Jeff probably didn't notice. Smiling, he had already turned his attention back to his machine. Focusing on my own, I flicked the power switch on the side and removed the roll from the box. Although I had been telling Jeff the truth, high school felt like forever ago.

Biting my lip, I set the microfilm on the wheel and tried to remember all the steps. When I went to place the edge of the film along the rollers, I realized it was upside down. Sighing, I turned it around, threaded it through the glass, and attached it to the wheel on the opposite end.

I pressed the advance button, and articles zoomed past the screen at a dizzying speed. Releasing the button, I focused the lens on the story in the center of the screen. It was from last Christmas. I glanced at the index card, then the label on the microfilm box. The articles on this roll would match the one I had already read online.

Frowning, I rewound the film and turned to Jeff. "We need to go back further."

He nodded. "I was thinking the same thing. There's a basket on the cabinet. Why don't you see how many boxes we can fit in it for now?"

THREE HOURS LATER, WE HAD FOUND OBITUARIES for all the dates on Lisa's list, along with a few others. After noticing a pattern, I had printed a few additional articles about women close to my age who had died. I knew some would be natural deaths, but there were plenty that weren't.

After searching through nearly half a century of newspapers, I had a small stack of printouts and an overfull basket of microfilm boxes. I also had an empty stomach.

As I placed the basket on the re-shelving shelf, I called over my shoulder to Jeff. "So, uh, what are your thoughts about lunch?"

He leaned his head over the back of his chair, rubbing his eyes with a sigh. "That it's long overdue. We done here?"

"Yeah. I need to read through these printouts. And read Lisa's story. Not sure which first."

Jeff switched off his machine and collected his own basket of microfilm boxes. "Lunch. Before all of that. But first, I need to show you something."

He returned his basket to the shelf before taking my hand and leading me back to the atrium. I frowned. He could have just asked me to follow him. Why was he holding my hand? And why didn't I seem to mind?

Jeff gave me no time to ponder this. As soon as we reached a staircase in the back corner of the room, he released me, indicating that I should go first. At the top, I saw study tables nestled between the stacks. There were also overstuffed armchairs that looked extremely comfortable. I didn't see anyone else up here and the quiet was peaceful.

Jeff again took my hand, guiding me to a window taller than me. It was tucked into the wall with a ledge large enough to sit upon. Judging by the knitted throw pillow resting in the corner, I had the impression many people *did* use this as a seat.

Jeff released my hand and gestured to the window, speaking in a voice just above a whisper. "Take a look."

Skeptical about why we were even here, I climbed onto the ledge and peered outside. I could see the entire town, as well as some boats in the distance. The sidewalks were bustling with tourists and the traffic below us was moving at a snail's pace. Without realizing it, I drew my knees to my chest, hugging them tight as I watched the scene below. It was mesmerizing.

"This was one of Lisa's favorite spots." Jeff took a step nearer, blocking me into the nook. Leaning close, he pointed over my shoulder.

"You can see my truck over there. Lisa liked to spend hours here. It was one of her favorite writing spots."

I nodded. "She told me about it. Wrote me letters from here."

I couldn't understand it when we were twelve, but now I could recognize this as an ideal place to people-watch. For a minute, I could almost imagine Lisa sitting beside me. I could stay here all day.

Except, my stomach had other ideas. When it growled, Jeff clapped his hands, rubbing them together as he smirked at me. "Lunch?"

Between the research and the visiting Lisa's favorite writing nook, I was a little too overwhelmed to speak.

Nodding, I followed Jeff back through the library in a reverent silence. Our footsteps echoed as we crossed the atrium.

The stillness was lost as soon as we stepped outside. Between the traffic and the tourists, it was difficult to hear myself think. It wasn't quite as crowded as home, but there were definitely a lot of people.

The buildings were all two-stories with the entryways inset, partially covering the sidewalks. Above each door hung a quaint sign displaying the name of the establishment.

I glanced at them as we passed. Beside the Belfort Bank was the Belfort Cinema. It actually looked like the theater might be above the bank, although I wasn't curious enough to ask Jeff. Unlike the multiplex where I grew up, this theater was only showing one movie, something I had seen two months ago. And hadn't enjoyed, despite all the hype.

Next to the cinema was a pub, but I wasn't surprised Jeff didn't want to stop in there. It felt too fancy, almost like a date. The sub shop beside it would be better.

But Jeff passed that as well, instead holding open the door to the *Pheasant Tidings*. The name sounded like a fancy restaurant and I really hoped he wasn't going to suggest I try the roasted pheasant. However, as I passed the window display, I realized we were entering a bookstore.

And it was adorable. Overstuffed chairs sat beneath the windows and at the endcap for each row of bookshelves on the side of the store. A small table on my right displayed books by local authors. Between it and the sales counter in the back was an area partitioned by waist-high shelves. I glanced over one to see small plush chairs for children surrounded by picture books.

The woman behind the counter waved. "Hey, Jeff. How's it going?"

He shrugged. "Can't complain. How's Mr. Hayes?"

The woman sighed. "Working too hard. And who's this?"

"Oh, this is Katie." He turned to me. "Katie? This is Mrs. Hayes. She owns the place. She was also my kindergarten teacher."

"That feels like forever ago." She winked at me before sending me a warm smile. "And what brings you here today?"

"I'm giving Katie a tour of the town. She's never been here before, but she was one of Lisa's best friends."

The woman's expression went from cheerful to sorrowful and back to a smile faster than I could blink. But I could feel the pity in the look. It made me uncomfortable.

Jeff seemed to feel the same way. He gestured to the store. "I was just showing Katie around a little. We, uh, better get going. Tell Mr. Hayes I say hi."

The woman nodded. "Yes, of course. It was good to see you."

As Jeff led me to the next store, I frowned. "Hey, Jeff? What was the point of stopping in there?"

He shrugged. "It was one of Lisa's favorite places. Mom used to work here. When we were younger, before Mom trusted Lisa in the library alone, she would bring us to work with her. Lisa spent hours curled up in those chairs writing."

I nodded. Lisa had told me in one of her first letters. She had also said how jealous she was that Jeff didn't have to stay in the store. I nudged him with my elbow. "And what'd you do?"

He gestured behind us. "I told my mom I was going to the library. But I would meet up with a friend who lived nearby, and we'd play video games all day."

Jeff and I joined a tide of people crossing the street to Beck's on the other side. I expected it to be a cheesy tourist shop, full of lobster and moose trinkets. I was surprised to find an old-fashioned soda fountain. A handful of black vinyl bar stools surrounded a chrome counter. The wall behind it was a giant chalkboard, listing dozens of ice cream flavors, some sandwiches, and even espresso drinks. In the center of the counter was a small sign announcing the area would open *around lunchtime.*

What kind of time was that? What if a person ate lunch early? Would they open earlier? And why were we even here if the restaurant was closed? I turned to ask Jeff, but he had disappeared.

Instead of tables for patrons, the opposite side of the store was lined with shelves full of the lobster and moose trinkets I had been expecting to see. Plenty of hats and shirts mixed in as well. But in the middle of the wall was a doorway connecting this store to the one beside it.

I walked through rows of summer sandals and flip-flops, as well as hiking and work boots, before emerging in a general store. I saw everything from housewares to toilet paper while I roamed around. A giant staircase in the center of the store led upstairs to office supplies and toys, as well as downstairs to garden and other outdoor essentials. I decided against exploring those areas.

As I emerged from a cereal aisle, Jeff reappeared. "So, what do you think?"

I glanced around. "Of what? It's a store."

Jeff shook his head. "No. It's Beck's. It's not just a store. It's an experience."

I rolled my eyes. I had seen that written on some of the shirts and mugs I had passed.

Jeff smirked. "Anyway, ready for lunch?"

I glanced around. "Where?"

He nodded his head toward the other room. "The soda fountain."

"But they're not open."

"Sure they are."

Jeff took my hand, leading me back to the counter. I had every intention of saying *I told you so* when he read the cryptic hours. But I didn't get the chance. The sign was gone. People were sitting on most of the stools. And a man wearing a white paper hat stood behind the counter, taking their orders.

I glanced between the store and the restaurant a few times. How long had I been browsing? And how did all these people seem to know when *about lunchtime* was?

Shaking my head, I sat beside Jeff at two of the stools and studied the overhead menu. A moment later, the guy behind the counter was standing before us.

"What can I get for you today?"

Since he was looking at me, I ordered first. "Can I get the Hannah Burger?"

"Fries?"

"Yeah. And, uh, a diet cola."

"No problem. And you?" The guy turned to Jeff.

He was smirking. "Same, but with a chocolate shake."

"Coming right up."

As the guy disappeared into the kitchen, Jeff nodded toward the menu. "The Hannah Burger is my favorite, not because of what's on it. I love that they named it after Hannah Cooper."

I frowned. "That name sounds familiar. I think Lisa mentioned her. Was she a friend of yours or something?"

Jeff laughed. "More like an obsession."

I bit my lip, leaning back a little on my stool. "Really?"

Jeff nodded. "When I was in sixth grade, we had to do a history report on someone famous from the area. Everyone was doing the founding fathers: Kensington, Middleton, Davenport. I wanted to be different. My teacher suggested Hannah Cooper."

"To help you?"

Jeff laughed. "No. As the subject of my report. She was a witch."

I raised my eyebrows. "Like, hocus pocus?"

"More like a misunderstood girl who was accused of being a witch in the eighteenth century."

"Salem witch trials."

Jeff's eyes glimmered with excitement. "Exactly. Except, here. Well, in Kensington. That's where our school was. Anyway, one day, the preacher's wife was said to have had words with Hannah. The next day, the woman walked off the lighthouse cliff and everyone believed Hannah had bewitched her."

"Did she?"

Jeff smiled. "You believe in the witches?"

I shrugged. "Not really. I was thinking maybe Hannah pushed her or something."

Jeff furrowed his brow. "I've never considered that. And I've been studying Hannah for years."

"What happened? Was she burned at the stake?"

Jeff nodded. "Yup. Witnesses claimed that as she burned, she laughed, saying she would be back. Several years later, another girl was accused of being a witch."

I shook my head. "She was probably just, like, socially awkward or something."

He shrugged. "Well, the townspeople thought Hannah's spirit had possessed her. They tried exorcisms and some other techniques, but strange things were still happening."

"So, they burned her?" I couldn't quite hide my disgust at the thought.

"Actually, that girl was hanged. And legend has it, Hannah's spirit has continued to pass from one young woman to the next for the past two hundred something years."

I rolled my eyes. "That's ridiculous."

Jeff shrugged. "Didn't say it was true. Just that's what people believe. I want to write a book about her someday."

I sent him a look of surprise. "I didn't realize you write."

"Not like my sister did. But I love researching. My senior project in college was about the colonial witch trials, with a special focus on Hannah Cooper. After I graduated, I joined the Kensington—"

Jeff's eyes went wide as he stared past me. I turned, making sure the ghost of Hannah Cooper wasn't behind me. Nothing was. Just the wall separating the restaurant from the kitchen. I turned back to Jeff.

"Katie, I'm sorry. I completely forgot."

"Forgot what?"

"I—"

"Order up." The waiter returned with a large tray. After placing plates in front of the couple beside us, he served me and Jeff our burgers and drinks. "Can I get you two anything else?"

Jeff shook his head. "Nah, we're good. Thanks."

My burger came topped with cheese and onion rings, as well as a special mayonnaise. I couldn't wait to try it. But Jeff still looked uncomfortable. I stared at him expectantly as he sipped his milkshake.

He frowned. "What?"

Picking up my burger, I shook my head. "You were telling me something about after you graduated."

Jeff nodded. "Oh. Yeah. When I moved to Kensington, I joined the local Historical Society."

"I thought you were part of the Copper Cove Historical Society. And the, what did you call it? Community Coalition?"

He laughed. "Community Council. And I am. I come home once a month for the meetings. I'm also on the Kensington Historical Society."

That still didn't explain why he looked as if he had seen a ghost. "Okay. So, why were you staring at me like you thought I was possessed by Hannah Cooper or something?"

He gave a small laugh. "Because I suddenly remembered that we have a meeting tonight to discuss the town's 350th anniversary celebration. Which means I've got to go to Kensington tonight. Well, probably all weekend. You're welcome to stay at the house, but if you'd like, you can come to Kensington. I can show you more of Lisa's favorite spots."

I waved a fry at him. "Lisa didn't have any favorite spots in Kensington. She didn't even like the library. The only thing she liked about it was the bus that brought her home after school."

Jeff frowned. "True."

"But I get your point. And, sure. I can come to Kensington. Did you want to leave as soon as we're done here?"

Jeff shook his head, swallowing his burger before answering. "Nope. We have time for one more stop."

THE LAST STOP TURNED OUT TO BE LIGHTHOUSE Point, where I had first visited when reaching Copper Cove. Jeff grabbed the shoebox before leading me to more or less the same spot I had sat the other night.

As we settled into the grass, Jeff gestured to the rocks. "Lisa loved it here. She would ride her bike, then lay here for hours, scribbling in her story notebooks."

I nodded. "I stopped here the other night. When I first came to town."

Jeff nodded, speaking more to the sea than to me. "Last night, I dropped a notebook, and it slid under the bed. When I went to grab it, I found this."

When he passed me the box, I sent him a curious look. "You brought me all the way out here to show me a pair of shoes?"

Jeff nudged my shoulder with his. "Just open it."

The lid was attached to the top of the box like a hinge. I flipped it open, finding a stack of envelopes inside. They were all addressed to Lisa. I recognized my own middle school handwriting with those strange-looking e's and i's dotted with little circles that never quite made it into hearts.

I turned back to Jeff. "These are all my letters to Lisa. Did you read them?"

He shrugged. "Only the top one. Once I realized it was from you, I figured they all were. Look at the top."

He pointed to the lid. I hadn't noticed it before, but Lisa had taped a list to the inside.

My favorite places I wish
I could share with Katie
- Library
- Bookstore
- Beck's Soda Fountain
- Lighthouse

I glanced out at the sea with tears in my eyes. Lisa hadn't been able to share these places with me. But Jeff had made sure I still experienced them.

When I spoke, my voice was as unsettled as the waves I continued to watch. "Thank you. For bringing me to all of Lisa's favorite places. I could feel her there. Here. I think she'd be thrilled you did that for her. You're a good brother."

He shook his head, his voice cracking. "I'm not."

"Why would you say that?"

"She was trying to tell me something, and I was too selfish to care. If I had just listened to her—"

I ran a hand along his arm. "Jeff, it wasn't your fault. And Lisa loved you. I don't think she would want you beating yourself up over her death."

Jeff nodded. "Maybe. I just wish I had some answers."

Grabbing the shoebox, I jumped to my feet. "Then let's go get some. While you have your meeting tonight, I'm going to read Lisa's story. I swear. The answers are in there somewhere."

I extended a hand, though I didn't actually expect Jeff to grab it. He held it a little longer than he probably needed to. Uncomfortable, I bit my lip and inclined my head toward his truck. "Should we be getting back?"

Jeff glanced out at the rocks one last time. "Yeah. Let's go find some answers."

Courtney looked at Stacey as they drank coffee on opposite sides of the small living room. "You know? You're the first person who's asked me about Allie. It's like she died and now all our friends forgot I'm still here."

Stacey bit her lip. "Maybe they just don't know what to say?"

"Or maybe they were never my friends in the first place."

Stacey took a sip from her mug. "I can't believe she's gone."

"I know, right? I keep expecting her to come down the hall in the middle of a conversation."

Stacey laughed. "Oh, man. I thought it was just me. She'd always come up to me in class, picking up a conversation that we had left off like three days ago. It always took me a minute to figure out what she was talking about."

"It was one of the things I loved best about her."

Stacey sighed. "I still can't believe she OD'd. I mean, I never would have thought she was into that kind of stuff. Did you have any idea she was using?"

"She wasn't. I mean, she never used to. But the past few weeks? She'd been acting really weird. Secretive. Did you know she was seeing someone?"

Stacey raised her eyebrows. "She was?"

Courtney nodded. "I wasn't supposed to know, but I overheard her talking to him on the phone one night. I got home early from choir and she didn't hear me come in. They were making plans for a weekend away."

"Oh! That sounds so romantic."

Courtney didn't agree. She looked like she had just sucked a lemon. "When I asked her about it, she told me I couldn't tell anyone. The guy was older. And married. They had to keep their relationship secret."

Stacey sipped her coffee. "You didn't approve."

Courtney shook her head. "My father had at least three affairs when I was a kid. Maybe more, but I only knew of three. Each time, he told my mother it would never happen again. But he couldn't help himself. I didn't want Allie getting hurt. The guy was bound to either break up with her or cheat on her."

Stacey screwed up her face in thought. "Maybe he did? I mean, maybe he hurt her, and she was so upset, she . . ." Stacey couldn't bring herself to say the words aloud.

Courtney shook her head slowly. "But where did she get the drugs to OD? It had to be from him. He must have gotten her hooked."

"Any idea who he was?"

"No clue. She never told me how they met or anything. All I know is that he was probably part of her department. She said they could talk about history forever."

Chapter 7

CARRYING A CANVAS BAG FULL OF GROCERIES, I followed Jeff up the flight and a half to his apartment. The place looked like it was built in the seventies. Outside had been a mixture of dark wood shingles mixed with aged brick. Inside, we made our way through hallways that may have once been orange but were now covered in decades of grime. As Jeff inserted his key into the doorknob of Apartment 207, I wondered if the interior was just as dated.

It wasn't. The room felt much brighter and more modern. I followed Jeff into the narrow kitchen, depositing the groceries on the counter and looking around. Other than the bags we had just brought, the place was immaculate. No dishes in the sink. No coffee stains on the laminate countertop. No magnets cluttering the fridge. I wished I could say the same of my place.

At the opposite end of the kitchen was a small dinette table for two. As I approached, I realized it opened to the living room. In the middle, a futon with a black cover faced a decently sized television on a stand made of the same wood veneer as the futon frame. A matching coffee table sat squarely between them.

Jeff entered the room from the other side of the kitchen. "Come on. I'll show you where you can sleep."

The hallway was short. I could see a darkened bathroom at the end. But he turned into the room on my left.

Although I had only had brief glances of Jeff's bedroom at the house, this room felt very similar and, again, I couldn't help comparing it to my own. While my walls held posters of various yellow smiley faces, Jeff's contained framed antique maps. I stepped closer, recognizing them as colonial-era sketches of Kensington, Copper Cove, and other area towns.

While my bed contained the same wrinkled sun-and-moon comforter I had used in college, Jeff's was a sleek black that was so straight, I wondered if he had ironed it after placing it over the mattress. In the corner of the room was a bookcase taller than me. Beside it sat a desk with a monitor and a full cup of pens.

As Jeff leaned over to turn on the CPU, I sent him a hesitant look. "So, uh, where can I sleep?"

He gestured behind himself, not bothering to turn away from the computer. "You can have the bed. I'll take the futon."

I bit my lip. "You sure? I don't mind the futon."

Jeff sent me a wide smile. "That's not how I was raised. You can have the bed."

"Thanks. So, uh, where's this meeting tonight?"

"Here. Otherwise, I probably would have skipped it."

I giggled. "You mean to tell me you're having a bunch of people over and you forgot?"

He shrugged. "It's been a busy week. So, should I make a veggie platter or just order a bunch of pizzas?"

I sent him an incredulous look. "That's not a serious question, is it?"

He nodded. "Yeah. I'll start cutting up some veggies."

I stared at him as he left the room. He was kidding, right?

THERE WASN'T TIME TO CUT ANY VEGETABLES. We had just unpacked the last bag of food when the buzzer sounded. Jeff went to the call box beside the door.

"Hello?"

"Hey, Jeff," squawked a voice. "It's Brian."

"Come on up." He pressed a button, creating another buzzing sound, before cracking open his apartment door and turning back to me. "I guess we'll have to order pizzas after all."

I just shook my head. Thankfully, he wasn't looking for an answer. He grabbed the phonebook from the shelf under the end table and brought it to the kitchen with the portable phone.

As he flipped through the pages, someone knocked on the door, opening it enough to enter. "Jeff?"

He didn't look up from the book. "In here." Pointing to the number with one hand, he dialed with the other.

The man who entered was so tall, he nearly had to stoop to avoid the doorframe. He was probably a little closer to thirty than I was, but not by much. His dark hair was cut short and, combined with his build, gave the impression that he might have been in the military.

He approached the kitchen with raised eyebrows. Jeff held up a finger. "Uh, yes. I'd like to place an order for delivery, please?"

Rolling my eyes, I exited the kitchen, gesturing for the newcomer to join me. "Hi. I'm Katie."

"Brian." He gave a small wave. "You, uh, new to the group?"

I bit my lip. How was I supposed to introduce myself? Jeff's dead sister's pen pal? That just sounded weird.

Thankfully, I was saved by the bell. Well, the door buzzer. Jeff held the phone to his chest. "Brian? Can you see who that is and buzz them in?"

The big guy nodded. "Yeah, sure."

Judy and Don arrived together, followed quickly by Phil, Rick, and Mark. By the time Carol came through the door, my head was swimming with names. Thankfully,

Jeff had finished ordering the pizzas and joined the group. While two of the men brought the dinette chairs to the living room, another man sat with the two women on the futon and the rest of us made ourselves comfortable on the floor.

Jeff stood. "Great. We're all here. Everyone, this is Katie. She's an old family friend who's visiting for a while."

The older woman smiled at me. "Do you share an interest in Kensington history as well?"

I bit my lip. "It's probably cool and everything. But, uh, I'm from Connecticut. I'm just here for the pizza."

Everyone laughed before the woman replied. "Well, I'm Judy Miller. My husband, Don, and I have been members for about thirty years. Since we're the oldest members, someone named us co-presidents."

One of the men in the chairs, who didn't look much younger, scoffed. "I believe that someone was you."

Judy shook her head. "Now, now, Phil. You're always welcome to take over."

Jeff clasped his hands loudly enough for everyone to turn their attention away from the arguing pair. Had that been his intention? His knowing smile suggested so.

"The pizza will be here in an hour. Let's see what we can accomplish before that. Judy?"

The woman nodded. "Yes, of course. So, let's start with the anniversary celebration." She glanced at me. "Kensington turns 350 next year. We're having a big to-do." She turned back to the group. "So, what should we do?"

Jeff looked around. "I think we should reenact some of the famous moments in Kensington history."

The younger of the two women, who still looked old enough to be my mother, nodded. "That's not a bad idea. What were you thinking?"

He shrugged. "Well, Hannah Cooper's trial is a favorite."

Brian pointed at him. "I don't think we can burn anyone at the stake. Not even a dummy."

I could see Jeff's disappointment as he nodded, but he forged ahead. "Well, there's the Kensington Tea Party."

I frowned. "Is that like the Boston Tea Party?"

His eyes were glittering with excitement again. "Yeah. See, Boston did it first, so they get all the attention. But a lot of other port towns followed their lead. Kensington dumped nearly twice as much tea as Boston. But because it was months later, we don't get mentioned in the history books."

The man on the couch shook his head. "Yes, but how would we reenact that? It's not politically correct to dress as Natives, and environmentalists would scream at us about polluting the harbor. Not to mention, what exactly would we dump?"

One of the men on the floor nodded. "Plus, we were hoping to keep the festivities near the center of town, not near the harbor."

Another guy pointed at Jeff. "I love the idea of reenactments. I really do. But think about this. Where are we going to find enough volunteers to perform them? How many times will they perform each one? Where would we get costumes and props and whatever?"

Jeff sighed. "Yeah, you all make good points. It was just an idea."

The old man in the chair, whose name might have been Phil, nodded. "It's a great idea, Jeff. And I think we should do it. Just not during the celebration."

Judy sent him a curious look. "What do you mean?"

Phil shrugged. "Well, as part of the celebration, we can have events every weekend over the summer. Different reenactments. One week can be the witch trial. Another the tea party. Do them several times a day. Same group of people. And we can contact some of the Boston groups to see how they do their reenactments."

The younger woman nodded. "I like that idea. But what about the actual celebration with the mayor?"

The man sitting in the other chair—Rick, maybe—snapped his fingers as he pointed to no one in particular. "What about tours of the historic landmarks? The lighthouse, the schoolhouse, the Middleton house?"

Everyone nodded, murmuring their agreement.

Except Judy. "It's a great idea, but I feel we need something bigger."

I glanced around. "I don't know about here, but my hometown is really big on parades. We have them for everything. We had a tricentennial a few years ago and all the different societies made floats. The first church in town, I think it was Congregational, but I could be wrong. They made two floats: one depicting the church when it was first built and one depicting it now, with the new steeple. A real estate office dressed up like colonists. A lot of local businesses took part, but all the floats had to be kept within the theme of the tricentennial."

The old man on the couch nodded, pointing at me excitedly. "Yes. Yes. I like this idea."

By the time the pizza arrived, the society had turned the parade into a solid idea, complete with subcommittees. When Jeff moved to a corner of the apartment with Phil and Rick, I followed them to see if I could assist with the planning of their task—deciding which historic landmarks should have tours and creating a script for each one.

Before we could get settled, Jeff disappeared to meet the delivery boy at the main entrance. Rick smirked in my direction. "We boring you yet?"

I smiled. "No. This is actually really cool. Makes me wish I had paid more attention to history in school."

Phil nodded. "I know the feeling. I nearly failed school when I was a student. Now, I write historic fiction. Go figure."

"Oh? You're a writer?"

Phil shrugged. "In my spare time. I'm also an English professor at Down East." He gestured to Rick. "We both are."

I raised my eyebrows. "You are? But isn't that in Southbridge?"

The professor shrugged. "That's just a couple of towns away. I don't live that far from here."

I bit my lip. "Jeff's sister, Lisa? She was a grad student at Down East."

Phil nodded slowly, his expression turning mournful. "I was her mentor."

I frowned. "Professor Norton?"

He smiled brightly. "You've heard of me?"

"Yeah. Lisa talked about you all the time. She was excited to have you as her advisor."

"You were close?"

I nodded. "I've known her forever. She's—I mean, she was—my best friend."

"I'm sorry for your loss." He looked around. "Did you know that Lisa's the reason I joined this group?"

I shook my head. "No. She didn't tell me that."

"True story. During our writer's retreat, I gave a seminar on writing historical fiction. Afterwards, we got to talking. When she learned I write stories about colonial witches, she insisted on introducing me to Jeff. He has a mild obsession with Hannah Cooper."

I smiled. "Yeah. I've heard."

"Well, it's an obsession we share." Phil nodded across the room. "Jeff introduced me to this group. He made it sound like everyone here was fascinated by the witch trials. But, mostly, it's just me and Jeff. I dragged Rick here."

Rick had been staring at a map of Kensington quietly. But at the sound of his name, he looked up. "Huh?"

Phil laughed. "I was just saying how I introduced you to the group."

Rick nodded. "He made it sound like everyone here is as obsessed with Wabanaki history as I am."

I made a face. "Waba what?"

"Wabanaki. The indigenous people who were here before the Europeans colonized."

"Oh. Okay." I looked around. "So, is that what most of you study?"

Rick shook his head. "No. Judy and Carol prefer the feminist and civil rights movements. Brian is all about the military. Don's just here because of Judy. But he used to be an accountant, so he makes a great treasurer."

I smiled politely, but Jeff returned with the pizzas. I rushed to the kitchen to give him a hand.

IT FELT LIKE FOREVER BEFORE THE APARTMENT was empty again. After Jeff promised to meet with Rick and Phil in the morning, he closed the door behind the professors and turned with a sigh.

"I'm so sorry. Our meetings never last that long."

I held up the stack of plates I was carrying to the kitchen. "It's because you fed them."

Jeff nodded. "Yeah. Lesson learned. Thanks for sticking around. You could have disappeared into the other room, you know."

I again raised the plates before setting them on the counter. "Again. Food."

Jeff laughed. "Well, I appreciate the company. It can be a little awkward being the youngest guy in the room."

I frowned. "That big guy. What was his name? He looked like he could have been in the army?"

"Brian? He's a weapons specialist in the National Guard. Or something like that."

I nodded. "Yeah, him. He didn't look that old."

"Turned forty last month. And was the youngest member of the Kensington Historical Society before I joined."

I giggled. "You two looked like you were having a serious discussion there for a while. He a Hannah Cooper fan, too?"

Jeff shook his head. "Military history. But we work together. He was telling me about one of his teammates quitting last week. There's a vacancy for a science teacher, if you're interested."

I gave a half laugh. "Yeah, right. I'm no teacher."

"Didn't you say you tutored?"

"Yeah, but that's just me helping kids with their homework."

Jeff waved a dismissive hand. "Teaching at a small school isn't that different. I mean, I was kidding about you applying here. But I kind of got the impression you weren't planning on being a coffee shop waitress for the rest of your life." He shrugged. "Something to consider when you drive back to Connecticut."

I left Jeff to clean the dishes and wandered to the bathroom to prepare for bed. *Back to Connecticut*. That felt strange to think about. I wasn't ready to go home. I still had so many unanswered questions here.

But, even when I found the answers, did I really want to leave? I had nothing waiting for me there. Sick of the New England weather, my parents and brother had all moved south. My friends had all scattered for college and none had returned. Most were in grad school. Some were pursuing careers in bigger cities.

There was no one waiting for me at home. As silly as it sounded, living with Jeff the past few days had felt comfortable. Maybe when I got back to Connecticut, I should look into getting a roommate.

Sighing, I returned to the bedroom. Roommates would have to wait. Right now, I had a stack of obituaries to read.

As Stacey crossed the campus, she couldn't help feeling paranoid. People greeted her. Waved. Nodded at her. Asked "How's it going?" But she could do no more than give a pathetic smile in return. Every eye that met hers, she wondered if they would be the next to die.

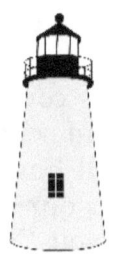

Chapter 8

"SO, DID YOU MAKE ANY PROGRESS LAST NIGHT?"
Jeff asked as he settled across from me at the dinette on
Friday morning.

Shaking my head, I sipped my coffee before replying. "I
was reading backwards. I fell asleep before Y2K."

Jeff gave a small laugh. "Well, you're welcome to hang
out here and read today if you want, but I would love to
show you around. I'm meeting up with Phil and Rick.
We're gonna do a walking tour of the landmarks. Decide
which we want on our tour."

I waved my fork in his direction. "Isn't the celebration
like a year away? Why are you putting forth all this effort
now?"

Jeff smiled. "A lot of reasons. First of all, we're aiming
to kick off the celebration Memorial Day weekend, so it's
only what? Like ten months? We need a plan in place so
we can create maps and pamphlets. Write scripts and get
actors for the reenactments. Costumes. All that stuff."

"Yeah, but you need ten months to do that?"

"The three of us are teachers, so we have more free
time now. Come August, we'll get too busy to spend more
than a few days a month working on this." Jeff smirked.
"Besides, I'd rather do all the walking around and stuff on
a gorgeous summer day than in the middle of winter."

I nodded. It was a valid point. But I had no response.
Instead, I thought about my plans for the day. I had none.
"Yeah, I guess I'd like to join you."

Jeff's smile seemed genuine. "Great. You can tell us
how bored you are."

When I sipped my coffee with raised eyebrows, Jeff winced.

"I meant, the three of us could drone on forever about boring stuff, like why the old schoolhouse has green paint or why the old meeting hall has a fireplace large enough to stand in. You can act as our typical tourist and let us know when we're boring you. Tell us which landmarks should and shouldn't be on our list."

I bit into my toast with a frown. "Do all the landmarks have informational signs? In my hometown, we have plaques and signs. *Meade House. Built 1742. George Washington stayed here during his march through Connecticut. Was used as a safe house in the Underground Railroad in 1850* or whenever."

"You memorized that?"

"No. I made it up. As an example. My point was, do your buildings have that?"

Jeff nodded. "Yeah. Mostly. The ones that don't, we can certainly look into making signs, even if they're temporary ones."

"Then what if you guys make a map? A self-guided walking tour."

Jeff tilted his head with a bemused expression as he finished the last few bites of his omelet. "That's not a bad idea. Judy's an artist. I bet she could draw something for us."

I sipped my coffee with a shrug. "Glad I could help. When did you want to leave?"

Jeff glanced at his watch. "An hour?"

I drained my mug. "Then I'm gonna jump in the shower. You mind if I leave you with this mess?"

Jeff smirked. "I've been cleaning up after you for days."

I smacked him on my way toward the bathroom. "Have not."

As I closed the door behind me, I thought about how easy things were between me and Jeff. I had only met him a few days ago, but it already felt as if I had known him forever. Lisa would be happy we were getting along so well.

Lisa. In all the hubbub about the celebration, I had forgotten my quest to figure out how she died. Should I be spending my afternoon reading her story and looking for clues instead of traipsing around town with her brother?

I turned on the water, letting it warm as I removed my clothes and considered my question. No. Lisa wouldn't want me obsessing. I had no doubt she'd like me to figure out what happened to her, but she would also want me to enjoy myself. After all, our annual trips to the Cape had been her way of making sure I didn't get lost in a biology lab.

If that were true, though, why did I feel so guilty?

I COULDN'T SHAKE THAT FEELING OF GUILT ALL day. I almost didn't climb into Jeff's truck. But I reassured myself that I was being ridiculous and tried to enjoy the sights as he drove to the historic district. Even though it was early, there were already plenty of tourists clogging the streets.

I was a little surprised when Jeff pulled into a drive beside a large stone sign that read *Kensington Regional Schools*. "I thought we were walking around the historical district."

Jeff shrugged. "Rick wanted to meet us here. Parking can be . . . difficult . . . this time of year."

I gave a half laugh. "Yeah, I can imagine. I live in a tourist town, too."

Jeff parked the car in the abandoned lot, opening the windows and killing the engine before turning to me with a smile. "You know? I've heard stories about you all my life, and I feel like I know you, but then you say things like that, and I realize I know nothing about you."

"Is that a good thing or a bad thing?"

He made a face. "Neither? Both? Makes me want to know more. Like, my sister was always saying you wanted to be a doctor. Didn't you used to read medical books as a kid?"

I laughed. "More like medical fiction. You know. Global outbreaks of deadly viruses. Doctors trying to save people with terminal illnesses. People in horrible accidents or being diagnosed with life-changing disorders and learning how they're going to adapt. That kind of stuff."

"And you read that as a kid?"

Biting my lip, I shrugged, unable to meet Jeff's eye. "Well, some were meant for kids. Well, teens." I could feel my face growing warm, and I didn't think it was the summer sun streaming into the truck.

Jeff grinned. "I spent most of high school reading novels about witch trials and colonial history. But if you had your heart set on medicine, why are you working in a coffee shop?"

I sighed. "When I was a freshman, I spent some time volunteering in a hospital, and I realized it wasn't really my thing. I tried the lab, but that wasn't really my thing either. I guess I like studying biology, but not really doing it."

"How'd you end up at the coffee shop?"

I shrugged. "It's near my apartment. They were hiring. It pays the rent. And I work mornings so I can spend my afternoons trying to figure out what I want to do with my life."

"Yeah. What'd you come up with?"

I bit my lip. "Well, you have to understand. *Everly Falls* is really addictive."

Jeff laughed. "And when you're done watching soap operas?"

"I spend most of my afternoons tutoring. Driving from one client to the next."

"What about now? Over the summer?"

I shrugged. "Still tutoring. Some SAT kids. Some summer enrichment."

"But you don't want to be a teacher."

I rolled my eyes. "This again?"

Jeff held up both hands in defense. "Just trying to get a picture." A car pulled alongside us, but he continued speaking as he turned the key in the ignition. "Have you ever asked yourself why you spend so much time tutoring? Just think about it. Hey, Rick."

I glanced out my window to see the professor climbing out of his car. "Hey Jeff." He pointed to me with a look of uncertainty. "Katie, right?"

I smiled. "You got it."

Grinning, he opened my car door. "So, where are we heading first?"

Since the professor looked like he was trying to climb on top of me, I slid along the bench closer to Jeff. Rick was not exactly a skinny man. While he wasn't that obese, he definitely held some girth. Enough to have me brushing my thigh against Jeff's.

I couldn't tell if I minded. Sure, it was a little uncomfortable being squeezed between the two men, but the one on my left smelled like the ocean. Or maybe I was simply inhaling the salt air coming through the window.

When Jeff shifted the car into gear, his arm rubbing against mine, I realized I hadn't been paying attention to their conversation. Not that it mattered. I probably wouldn't have recognized where we were heading, anyway.

As Jeff drove through the town, he or Rick would point to random landmarks and say their names. Neither said why it was important, but they both must have known because Rick noted each in the steno pad he held in his lap. Most were houses, although there were also a couple of churches and a statue of some old guy standing in the middle of what I could only assume was the town green. Jeff circled it a few times before parallel parking nearby. As Rick climbed out of the truck, Jeff turned to me with a smile.

"Got your walking shoes on?"

I held up a foot the best I could. "Ready and rearin' to go."

"Then let's go introduce you to Historic Kensington."

I followed Rick and Jeff to the statue. The old guy was some generic Civil War soldier. On his plinth were the names of the men and women who had died fighting in the Civil War and both World Wars, as well as the Korean and Vietnam Wars.

I turned to Jeff. "No offense, but this statue is like the one in my hometown. And I'm willing to bet every hometown in the nation. What makes this one so special that people on your walking tour are going to be dying to come here?"

Phil approached with a laugh. "Well, it's not the memorial, but the common itself. Back when the town was chartered, the founding families built their houses around this parcel of land. They used it for public gatherings and military training. The people of the town would allow their livestock to graze here."

I nodded. "Like every other town green in New England. I mean, it's cool and all, but it's kind of boring."

Jeff smiled. "Well then, let's just use this as a starting point. Where to first?"

The two professors glanced at the surrounding buildings. Rick pointed to the opposite side of the common. "Brown House?"

Jeff nodded. "Sounds good."

I followed the men to a two-story brick building. There was nothing unique about it. It looked like many other houses I had seen growing up.

Phil pulled out a ring of keys large enough to make a high school janitor jealous, muttering to himself as he flipped through them.

I turned to Jeff. "This is probably a stupid question, but why is it called the brown house if it's made of brick?"

Jeff laughed. "Well, this is the oldest brick house in the county. The Brown family built it in 1805. Most houses were wood frame until the end of the century."

"Aha!" Phil held a key above his head. "Found it." After unlocking the door, he stood on the threshold and gestured us inside.

We stepped into the main hall, which was dimly lit. On our right was a staircase leading to an even darker second story. To the left was a large entrance to a room with light pouring in from the windows. I gravitated toward it. Not that there was much to see. It was empty. The floor was made of wide slats of a wood that was probably dark at one time, though it looked almost white in the thin layer of dust coating it. Along one wall was a fireplace nearly as tall as me. It opened into the room behind. Through another doorway, I could see that room was also empty.

I turned to the men, who were still standing in the hallway. "So, uh, other than the fact that this house is brick, is there anything else special? Because, in my opinion, it's kind of creepy."

Rick frowned. "Well, I don't know about creepy. But it *would* take a lot of effort to get this house ready by next year. We'd need to scrub it clean. Not sure if there are electric lights. Then we'd have to furnish it."

Jeff sighed. "But this is a really cool house. And there are lights. I've toured this house before. I bet Anderson's would have the furniture we need."

I glanced between the men. "Is Anderson's another house?"

"Nah. An antique store in the next town."

Phil made a face. "That's gonna be expensive. Tell you what. Let's take a quick tour. Make sure there's nothing living here—"

I could feel my eyes grow wide. "Living here?" My voice was definitely an octave higher than it should have been.

Laughing, Jeff put an arm around my shoulder, drawing me a little closer with a squeeze. "Relax. I'm sure it's fine."

With Jeff holding me, I felt slightly braver. I nodded. "Yeah. You just surprised me, that's all."

Thankfully, my voice was no longer shaky. Unfortunately, as soon as Jeff released me, my bravado disappeared with his arm.

I glanced around. "It's, uh, a little stuffy in here. If it's okay with you guys, I think I'll go take a look outside while you're checking for ghosts or whatever."

Jeff smirked as I scurried out the front door. I knew he didn't believe me. Especially since, if anything, the building felt air conditioned compared to the outside. But I didn't care. It wasn't like I was afraid of ghosts. It was the idea that there might be something living upstairs. Such as mice. Or a raccoon. Or bats.

Shuddering, I walked around the building, expecting the grounds to be overrun. But they were impeccable. Flowers were blooming in a neatly tended garden in the backyard. Fruit was growing from trees along the side. Apples, pears. Even peaches. They looked delicious.

But nothing was ripe. Besides, the idea of grabbing one felt like trespassing. I circled around the building, returning to the front as the men emerged.

Jeff smirked at me. "You will be happy to learn we found no ghosts."

I pursed my lips. "What about four-legged creatures? Or winged ones?"

"Well, there was that large bat in the attic. Could have been a vampire."

Rick shook his head. "Stop scaring the poor girl. There were no bats. Or any other creature bigger than a spider. But it would still take a lot of effort to get that house presentable in ten months."

Jeff pointed to a white Federalist-style building across the way. "Norton House?"

Phil nodded excitedly. "Definitely."

I raised my eyebrows at him. "Norton? Like your house?"

He laughed. "My ancestors. It definitely needs to be on the tour."

I glanced between the two men as we walked along the common. "Why?"

Phil gestured to Jeff with a look of incredulity. "You're friends with this guy, so I know you know the story of Hannah Cooper. She killed the preacher's wife."

"Allegedly," interrupted Jeff.

A look passed over Phil's face. A malevolent glare. Was he angry that Jeff thought Hannah could be innocent? Why?

I blinked, and the look was gone. Had I imagined it? I glanced at Jeff beside me. He seemed unfazed. Possibly even amused. I turned back to Phil on my other side. He was looking at me expectantly.

What was the question? "Uh, yeah. I know the story."

Phil pointed at the white house. "This was where the Nortons lived." He gestured to the Civil War statue. "The first Hannah was killed over there."

I sent him a curious look. "The first Hannah?"

"Yeah. When she was burned at the stake, her spirit moved to another girl. That girl was eventually hanged, but her spirit moved on again. It's been traveling from young woman to young woman for centuries."

I wanted to laugh. Something akin to a snort made its way out of my mouth before I realized Phil wasn't kidding. I sent him a skeptical look. "You honestly believe a witch's ghost has been possessing girls for over three hundred years?"

Rick shook his head. "Oh, don't get him started on that."

Somehow, Jeff had moved to the other side of Phil. Since the professor was looking at me, he couldn't see Jeff twirling a finger beside his ear to indicate he thought the older man was crazy.

Phil nodded. "Yes. Every time a Hannah dies, her ghost moves on to someone else."

I chose my words carefully. "But how can you be so sure?"

"Because I've met her. Many times. She killed the love of my life."

Rick groaned. "Not this again. For thirty years, I've been listening to this story." He turned to me. "I told you not to get him started."

There was something about Rick's annoyed expression that made me uncomfortable. Thankfully, we had reached the Norton House. While Phil searched through his key collection, I inched closer to Jeff.

I made sure he was standing between me and Rick for the rest of the day.

Stacey lay awake in her bed, staring at the moon shining through her open window. She couldn't sleep. Her mind was racing, thinking about her investigation. She was getting close to an answer. She could feel it in the pit of her stomach. Women were dying on campus and it wasn't a drug overdose. Something was killing them.

Stacey sat bolt upright. What if it wasn't a something? What if it was a someone?

The idea was too horrible to fathom. A serial killer? At her school? Surely not. Someone would have figured it out by now.

But as Stacey returned her head to her pillow, she felt a flutter in her stomach. There was a person responsible for the death of all these women. She was certain of it.

And she was determined to find out who.

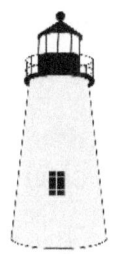

Chapter 9

I SPENT THE REST OF THE MORNING WALKING through town with the historical society nerds. After the two homes, we examined the old opera house. Since it was currently operating as a playhouse, we voted to add it to the walking tour, but not use it for reenactments.

The library was another historic landmark that would not easily accommodate performances. The old schoolhouse would be fantastic if they could get some child volunteers.

By the time we returned to the truck, I was starving. I said as much as I slid into my seat.

Jeff glanced at the other men. "What about the lighthouse?"

I groaned. "Seriously. Before we look at another landmark, I need to eat something."

Jeff shrugged. "Two birds. One burger."

I didn't have a clue what he meant, but the other men must have.

Rick nodded. "I'm game."

Phil shook his head. "I've got to pass. I have a meeting at the university this afternoon."

Waving to Phil, Jeff and Rick piled into the truck. While they debated having a reenactment at the lighthouse, I leaned as close to Jeff as possible without sitting in his lap. Since he said nothing, I assumed he hadn't noticed.

But he had.

The lighthouse was at the end of the peninsula, where the road ended in a large lot. The park was bigger than the one in Copper Cove, as was the lighthouse, which was attached to a two-story home.

Jeff pointed to it as he parked. "Maybe instead of reenactments, we can do demonstrations on how they used to run the light before electricity."

Rick nodded. "That's an idea. I'm gonna hit the head. I'll meet you at the Shipwreck."

As the professor climbed out of the truck, I turned to Jeff with raised eyebrows. "Shipwreck? That sounds like something that should be on your tour."

Jeff smirked. "Yeah, except it's just the name of the snack bar. Are you okay?"

"Yeah. Why?"

His face turned red, and I didn't think it was from walking in the summer sun all morning. "You were just sitting kind of close. I mean, I don't mind. But it's just—"

His babbling only made his face turn more red. I tried to smile. "I can't explain it. It's just, there's something about Rick that makes me uncomfortable. It's not something he did or said or anything. Just ... this feeling."

Jeff smiled. "Okay. I mean, I'd rather you be comfortable, but if he's making you nervous, then I don't mind."

I sent him a weak smile. "Thanks."

I could see Rick exiting the men's restroom. I gestured to him. "You said something about a shipwreck?"

Jeff smiled. "You should try the *Mayday Margaret*."

I climbed out of the truck, sending him a skeptical look as he met me near the front. "What is that?"

"You'll see. And you'll love it."

The *Mayday Margaret* turned out to be a grilled chicken sandwich named after a ship that had wrecked in the early twentieth century. It wasn't bad, and I wanted to enjoy it. Unfortunately, it wouldn't go down easily. Being near Rick was creating knots in my stomach.

The worst part was, I really couldn't explain why. The more I tried to avoid it or convince myself I was being irrational, the more my stomach revolted.

It probably didn't help that Jeff once again brought up Hannah Cooper. "They found Hetty Norton over there." He pointed to a small cove between our picnic table and the lighthouse. "According to a witness, she walked right off the cliff. Broke her neck on the rocks below."

I shuttered. Even though I had only eaten half my sandwich, my appetite was gone. I pushed it away.

Jeff sent me a concerned look. "You didn't like it?"

I tried to smile. "No, it was fine. I'm just not that hungry."

"Can I finish it?"

I shrugged. "Be my guest."

Sliding my plate toward himself, Jeff continued babbling about his lifelong obsession.

"At the trial, Hannah said she knew Hetty was planning to jump off the cliffs and Hannah was trying to convince her otherwise. Said that's why they had argued after Sunday Service. But the entire town was already convinced she was a witch."

Rick looked annoyed. I knew I was getting a little sick of hearing about a three-hundred-something-year-old witch.

Hoping to distract him, I turned to Jeff. "So, you said you wanted to show how they lit the lantern without electricity. How would you do that? I mean, I'm assuming you can't use the real lighthouse."

Shaking his head, Jeff pointed to an outbuilding. "We still have the old light."

Rick nodded. "That shed is probably big enough to hold a small tour."

I frowned. "That's great and all, but do you have anyone that *knows* how to do it?"

Jeff sent me a sheepish look. "I, uh, hadn't considered that. I'm not sure."

Rick appeared lost in thought. "Isn't Don on the lighthouse preservation committee? He may know someone."

"And I can ask Brian. Maybe one of his sciencey friends would know."

Thankfully, the men didn't need to tour the lighthouse. Within a few minutes, they had a full plan for how to incorporate this landmark in their celebration.

We once again climbed into the truck and I squeezed close to Jeff. He sent me a quick smile before leaning past me.

"So, Rick. I think we've got a good starting place. Think we need to hit any more landmarks?"

The professor shook his head. "No. I feel good about our plan."

We returned to the school to deposit Rick at his car. As I slid back to the passenger seat, Jeff muttered something under his breath.

I glanced at him. "Sorry. I didn't catch that."

Jeff smirked. "I was saying you didn't have to move over. Anyway, what should we do this afternoon?"

I sighed. "I really want to look through those printouts. Maybe keep reading."

"But it's such a gorgeous day. Wouldn't you rather go to the harbor or something?"

"Honestly? No." I sighed. "I know Lisa died months ago and you probably want to just move on. And I get that. I respect that. But, to me, Lisa's death is still new, and I need answers. Something just isn't sitting right with me. If you don't want to do this with me, I completely understand. But I'm not going to be able to accept Lisa's death until I learn why."

Jeff placed a hand on mine and looked like he wanted to say something. But his expression changed as he removed it. "Rick? Everything okay?"

Sliding closer to Jeff, I glanced out the open window. The professor was pressed against my door.

His knowing look made me feel guilty. Like he had caught Jeff and me doing something more than talking. Uncomfortable, I moved even further away from the man.

He smirked. "Hey. Sorry to interrupt you two. I can't find my phone. Is it on the floor or something?"

Jeff grabbed the one on his dash. "I'll call it. What's the number?" He pressed the buttons as Rick rattled it off.

A moment later, the professor's pants were singing. He held up the phone with a sheepish smile. "Guess I had it all along. Thanks. I'll talk to you later."

With a wave, he climbed into his car. I again returned to my seat, but Jeff waited until Rick left before starting the truck.

We rode back in silence. I didn't know what was running through Jeff's mind, but I was wondering what he had been about to say before Rick had interrupted him. I was dying to know. But too chicken to ask.

WHEN WE ARRIVED AT THE APARTMENT, JEFF made a beeline to the bathroom. I searched through the papers I had brought from Copper Cove. I had packed Lisa's overnight bag with her manuscript and anything else I thought might come in handy. Where had I stowed the obituary printouts?

I searched the bag twice. I couldn't find them. Jeff entered the room as I was emptying the contents of the bag onto the bed for a third time.

"Everything okay?"

"I can't find the obituaries."

"Weren't you reading them last night?"

I stopped my frantic search, my face growing warm. "I forgot." Glancing at the pillows, I tried to remember what I had done last night. I had been reading until my eyes grew heavy. I had wanted to keep the papers safe, so I put them . . . where?

In the nightstand. As I pulled open the drawer, Jeff let out a weird noise. Something like a gasp and a screech, but barely audible. When I turned to see if he was okay, his eyes were wide and his face flushed.

He pointed to the nightstand. "You don't need to go in there."

"Yeah. It's where I stored the papers last night."

I removed the stack and immediately understood Jeff's embarrassment. Condoms littered the drawer. I picked up one that had dropped by my feet.

"Sorry. I didn't see them last night. Seriously, though. It's no big deal. I have the same thing in my nightstand."

Jeff looked amused. "You do?"

I shrugged. Since I wasn't seeing anyone and didn't do one-night stands, my drawer wasn't nearly as full as his. But I wanted to reassure him. "Yeah. Of course. Who doesn't? Anyway." I held up the obituaries to change the subject. "Shall we?"

Jeff and I settled on the living room floor, the coffee table between us. He took the first one from the stack.

"So, what exactly are we looking for?"

I frowned. "Dunno. I guess, first of all, we need to figure out if Lisa knew any of these people. Then maybe see if they have something in common."

Jeff nodded. "Well, this one grew up in Augusta, but she was a student at Down East. She may have known Lisa."

I took the sheet, reading through it as Jeff consulted the next obituary. The article mentioned this student was an English major. She was an undergraduate, but that didn't mean much. Lisa may have still shared a class or group with her.

I placed the page aside and looked at the next one on the stack. The woman was around the same age. She had also been a student at Down East University at the time of her death. She had been a psych major and died while Lisa was still in high school. I doubted they knew each other.

But the school was a connection. Something the two women had in common. I placed the second obituary on top of the first.

By the time Jeff and I had read through all the printouts, we had divided the papers into two groups. The list of people who had attended Down East University was nearly as big as the stack of people who hadn't.

I shook my head. "This can't be a coincidence."

Jeff frowned. "I know. But what does it mean? Is there something in the water making everyone want to go kill themselves?"

"Maybe a teacher is driving them all to depression?"

Jeff's expression turned mournful. "You don't think . . . Could Lisa have grown so depressed that she—"

I reached over the table to place a comforting hand on his arm. "No. I refuse to believe Lisa killed herself."

"Maybe school had gotten to be too much."

I shook my head. "I studied a little about suicide in one of my classes. Did you know only a small percentage of people leave notes? But Lisa? She's the kind of person who would have left one."

Jeff sent me a hesitant look. "You don't think . . . her story? Could that have been a really long suicide letter?"

I sighed. "I mean, it's possible. But think about how long it took her to write that. She would have had to have been *really* depressed for a *really* long time. And we would have known. But—" I got to my feet. "I guess there's only one way to find out. I'll go grab it."

Jeff stood as well. "I'll start dinner. I'm hungry. How's pasta with sauteed vegetables sound?"

"Amazing."

Jeff smiled. "Two amazings, coming up."

As he headed to the kitchen, I raced to the bedroom. I knew exactly where to find Lisa's story. I had unpacked it three times when I was searching for the obituaries. While Jeff busied himself in the kitchen, I settled myself on the futon.

Oh, Lisa. What secrets did you leave for me?

Stacey glanced at the index card in her palm. Allie Edwards. Turning to the filing cabinet, she flipped through the folders in the top drawer until she found the transcript. She grabbed the records on either side of Allie's before crossing the room to the scanner.

Accepting the job in the registrar's office was pure genius, Stacey thought as she placed the file on the glass. She had unlimited access to the records she needed, all under the guise of digitizing transcripts of former students.

As the files scanned, Stacey inserted a floppy disk into the computer. Before entering Allie's information into the transcript program, she saved a copy of the scan onto her disk. It would take a few days, but Stacey was confident she'd be able to find the records of all the girls who had died in the last dozen years.

And then the real investigation could begin.

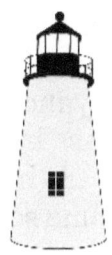

Chapter 10

I SAT UPRIGHT WITH A START, FROWNING AS I reread the last few lines of the chapter. They weren't sitting well with me. "Jeff?"

He responded from the kitchen. "Yeah?"

"Didn't Lisa take a part-time job at the registrar's office?"

He peeked out around the kitchen wall to frown at me. "Yeah. So?"

"Did she tell you why?"

"She wanted a little extra cash to feed her coffee addiction. Why?"

"What if it was a cover story?"

Jeff put down the knife he was holding before wiping his hands on a towel and giving me his full attention. "What are you talking about?"

I held up the manuscript. "Lisa's story. Stacey gets a job at the registrar's office so she can snoop through student records. What if Lisa did the same thing?"

Jeff sent me a skeptical look. "That doesn't sound like my sister."

"I know. But she had a floppy disk in her container labeled *transcripts*."

"So? I do too. It's my college transcripts. Because I was considering applying to grad school."

I huffed out a breath. Why couldn't Jeff see what I was seeing? "I thought the same thing. But what if they weren't her transcripts? What if they belonged to other people?"

"So, you want to go back to the house just to look at a floppy disk?"

I could hear the annoyance in his voice. I almost understood why. This was his home. When he had emptied the other fridge, I had assumed he had no intention of returning anytime soon.

But I wasn't asking him to. I shook my head. "Nah. I figured there might be a disk in there that would be helpful, so I grabbed the whole caddy. It's in my bag." I gestured to the bedroom. "Can we use your computer?"

Picking up the knife, he nodded toward the hallway. "Knock yourself out."

It was still on from yesterday. I returned Lisa's overnight bag to the bed and unearthed the floppy disks, bringing the entire caddy to the desk. Settling into Jeff's chair, I flipped through the box. In the middle was the one labeled *transcripts*.

My hands were shaking as I inserted the disk into the drive. Why? It wasn't like Lisa had left a hidden message on the floppy.

I found myself holding my breath as the disk loaded. But Jeff had been right. These were just Lisa's transcripts.

I sat back with a sigh. I had been so sure I would find answers here. My eyes landed on Jeff's CD collection near his bed. Curious, I went to see what it held. A lot of alternative, just like me. Some hard rock, which wasn't quite my style, but something I could tolerate. Definitely no country.

Smiling to myself, I remembered the CDs I had left in Jeff's truck. I glanced at the computer. Maybe Stacey's playlist would play on it.

With a shrug, I went back to the kitchen. "Hey. Can I borrow your keys?"

Jeff sent me a skeptical glance. "What's wrong with your car?"

I rolled my eyes. "I left something in your truck. Mind if I go grab it?"

He nodded. "Yeah, sure. Any luck with the transcripts?"

I shook my head. "No. You were right. It was just Lisa's."

Jeff sent me a sympathetic look. "It was a good try, though." He gestured to a hook near the door. "Keys are there."

I took them with a smile. "Thanks."

The CDs had fallen into the space between the seats and the back window. I had to crawl around to find the one I wanted. Making sure I locked the truck behind me, I returned to the building.

Curiosity was getting the better of me. I really wanted to hear this playlist now. After replacing Jeff's keys on the hook, I went back to the bedroom. I inserted the CD before I even had a chance to sit.

Once again, I was met with disappointment. There was no music on here. The CD opened to reveal a number of files. Judging by their extensions, they were images. They didn't have real names. Just a bunch of random letters and numbers, although, looking carefully, I did notice a pattern to them.

I clicked on the first one. It was a transcript. But it wasn't Lisa's. It belonged to a girl named Sarah Johnson. She had attended Down East University in 1994 and had a decent GPA. Judging by her courses, she was probably a science major. But she had taken a few classes in other departments. And never graduated.

I clicked on the next image. I recognized the name on the transcript from my pile of obituaries. She was a student who had died a year after Sarah. Lots of business classes. But she had taken a multidisciplinary honors course. My eyes fixated on the name of the professor. It had been on Sarah's transcript as well.

I hurriedly clicked on the rest of the images. It was a coincidence, right? The university wasn't that big. Of course, two students would have the same professor.

But as I scanned each transcript and continually found the name, a lead weight settled in my stomach. By the time Jeff leaned over the back of my chair, I thought I might throw up.

"What'd you find?"

I gestured to the computer. "That CD that wouldn't play yesterday?" My voice sounded scratchy and far away. I couldn't eek out any more words. Instead, I pointed to the screen.

Jeff peered over my shoulder. "It was transcripts? Whose?"

I went back to the folder. There had to be fifty images, though most of the transcripts were two or three pages long.

Jeff let out a low whistle. "That's a lot of students."

I nodded. When I spoke, my voice was barely a whisper. "They all had the same professor."

Jeff sent me a surprised look. "Really? That can't be a coincidence, can it? Who was it?"

I opened a random file, scrolling to the History 101 listing. I pointed to the professor.

Richard Sanderson.

Jeff blanched. "Katie, you know who that is, don't you?"

I shook my head. "No, but I don't think Lisa had him. I double checked her transcripts."

Jeff sighed. "Katie, this is Rick. Lisa knew him. He taught a writing historical fiction workshop last summer. But, you don't seriously think—"

"That Rick is responsible for over a dozen deaths? I really, *really* hope not. But it's a big coincidence."

Jeff leaned over me, taking the mouse from my hand. I said nothing. He needed to see for himself, though it frustrated me that he didn't believe me. He was practically crushing me.

While Jeff searched, I tried to make sense of it all. There were two possibilities. Either there was something about Rick and his class that was driving people to suicide or—I didn't want to consider the alternative.

I knew the second Jeff came to the same realization. His hand slackened on the mouse and his body collapsed a little more into mine. I turned around, our noses only inches apart.

"You okay?"

He shook his head, his face pale. "He's my friend. Well, a colleague. How . . . how does Lisa fit into this?"

I bit my lip. "I haven't really thought about it. We need to figure out what it is about Rick and his class that fifteen girls have died. Then maybe we'll figure out Lisa's role."

Jeff was still shaking his head. "It has to be a coincidence. I mean, maybe the classes he's taking are mandatory, so it's just a coincidence. Like, if fifteen kids from Kensington High School suddenly died, you would say they all had me as a history teacher at some point."

I nodded. "That's entirely possible." Though college differed from high school, and I didn't believe it was as likely a scenario as Jeff was saying. But I wanted it to be true, too. The thought that it was anything more than coincidence was difficult to swallow.

I figured it was time to change the subject. "Hey. Why don't we forget about it for now? Have something to eat and then—"

Jeff stood quickly enough to give himself whiplash. Swearing, he raced out of the room.

What did I say? He wasn't *that* hungry, was he?

As I approached the kitchen, I was hit with the smell of charred . . . Something. I wasn't sure what. The mess in the pan was burned beyond recognition. Jeff kicked the garbage can as he tried to pry the blackened remains from the pan.

I put a hand on his shoulder. "Tell you what. Let me handle this. I'm a pro. I do this on a weekly basis. You go find a place where we can order out. We'll grab a case of beer and forget about this horrible situation for the night."

Jeff nodded. "Sounds good to me. But leave the pan."

I smiled. "No. Seriously. I'm a pro. Campus fire department visited me on a monthly basis because I kept setting off the smoke alarm in my apartment."

I hadn't been kidding, but it was enough to bring a small smile to Jeff's lips. While he searched the phone book for a restaurant, I used a spatula to scrape as much of the ruined dinner from the pan as I could. Then I rifled through the cabinets for the salt shaker, dumping a generous amount onto the mess and massaging the crystals into the bottom of the pan. By the time I set it in the sink to soak, Jeff had returned to the kitchen.

"Okay. I got pizza, six different seafoods, or Chinese."

I didn't need to consider it. "Definitely Chinese."

Nodding, Jeff placed the phonebook on the counter beside me, leaning close to point at the full-page menu advertisement. "What sounds good?"

I followed his finger, but it took a moment to read the words. I was having trouble focusing with Jeff so close. What did he ask me?

Oh yeah. I read the menu a couple of times before deciding on the chicken lo mein. While Jeff wandered back to the living room to call in the order, I quickly raided the cabinets. One of them had to have liquor.

Yes. The one beside the fridge. Not that there was a wide selection. But Jeff had my favorites: rum, vodka, and coffee liqueur. There was easily enough for us to have several drinks. I still intended to pick up a case of beer, but I wanted to know the hard stuff was around as a backup. It was going to take a lot of drinks to forget what we had learned about our investigation.

Jeff returned to the kitchen, smiling when he saw the open cabinet. "Great minds think alike. I ordered delivery so we could get nice and wasted while we're waiting."

I gestured to the cabinet. "What'd you have in mind?"

"Well, I have a case of beer in the fridge, but I'm thinking I need a gin and tonic. You?"

"Not really sure. Something with the coffee liqueur, I think."

Jeff nodded. "Got it. I'll play bartender. Why don't you go turn on the game?"

I frowned. "What game?"

Jeff looked at me like I had two heads. "Sox? Versus Yankees? *Is* there any other game?"

"Oh. Yeah, I guess. I'm not that into baseball."

Jeff shook his head mournfully. "You poor girl. Go switch it on. Channel 45. It's gonna be a great game."

THE COMBINATION OF LO MEIN, ALCOHOL, AND baseball made it almost possible to forget the connection between my best friend's death and her professor. By the third inning, I had a pleasant buzz. One of the Yankees stepped up to the plate. As he hit the ball, I heard a similar crack next to me. Glass shattered as a baseball came flying toward me.

I dove out of the way. Beside me, Jeff did the same. My heart in my chest, I stared at the window. At the hole a little larger than my fist. On the floor beneath, in a pile of broken glass, sat a baseball. A paper was wrapped around it. I could see something scrawled on it, though I couldn't read what it said from where I was.

I turned to Jeff. "What was that?"

He shook his head as he inched toward the window, careful to avoid the shards on the floor. "I don't . . . I don't know. Maybe some kids were playing in the parking lot?"

"Do you see any?"

"No. They could've run away."

Biting my lip, I shook my head. "I don't know about you, but I never played baseball with a note tied around the ball. I don't think this was an accident. Do you think maybe we should call the cops?"

Jeff turned to me with a sigh. "Yeah. Probably." He carefully picked his way around the glass to cross the living room. "Should we read the note?"

I frowned. "I don't know. Maybe they'll want to test it for fingerprints or something."

Jeff nodded absently as he dialed the phone. "Yeah. That's a good point."

It took forever for the police to arrive. By the time red and blue lights flashed through the window, the Yankees had finished their half of the inning and the Sox were at bat.

Jeff went to the main entrance to greet the police, leading an officer to his apartment. The man looked old enough to be my father and had a gut that suggested he spent a lot of time at the doughnut shop.

Jeff must have explained the situation in the hallway, because the officer was carrying a small bag. As soon as they entered, Jeff pointed to the baseball.

"It's right over there. We didn't want to touch anything until you arrived."

The officer nodded, pulling a disposable camera from his bag. After taking a few shots, he swapped it for a glove and plastic bag. As he picked up the ball, he glanced at Jeff.

"There's something wrapped around this. Looks like a note."

Jeff nodded. "We figured we'd let you read it for us."

The policeman smirked. "Been watching crime shows on tv?"

Jeff shrugged, and I could feel my face grow warm. Now that the officer said it, I felt ridiculous. But he made no further comments, unwrapping the paper and reading aloud.

"*Lisa is at peace. Leave her be. Stop investigating or you'll join her.*" The officer turned to Jeff. "Any ideas what this means?"

Jeff had grown pale. Honestly, I wasn't feeling much stronger. I braced myself against the futon. A death threat? How did anyone even know we were looking into Lisa's accident in the first place?

The officer was staring at us expectantly. I did my best to explain. "Jeff's sister, Lisa. She, she passed away. A few months ago."

The officer nodded. "Was it a natural death?"

I shrugged. "She was found on the rocks near the Copper Cove lighthouse."

The officer held up the note, which was now in the plastic bag with the rock. "This says you're investigating. Is her case still open?"

Jeff shook his head. "No. I . . . I don't know what that note means. We're not investigating anything."

"Any idea why someone might think you are?"

I tried not to make eye contact. It was a great question. One I couldn't answer.

Jeff shrugged. "No clue. We were just trying to watch the ball game."

The officer glanced at the screen. "Sox ahead by one? Awesome." He turned back to us, holding up the plastic bag. "I'll take this in, but I'll be honest. There's not much to go on here. Any idea who could have sent this?"

I had a lot of ideas. None of them made enough sense to voice aloud. I shook my head. Jeff did the same.

The officer stayed for a while, asking some more questions and taking a few last photos before knocking on doors to interview the other people in the building. Jeff and I had just finished sweeping the glass when the officer returned.

"None of the neighbors saw anything. I'll keep you informed if we find out anything." He passed us each a business card. "If you think of anything else, call me."

Nodding, I slid the card into my jeans. Jeff walked the officer outside, bringing the bag of broken glass to the dumpster. While he was gone, I frowned at the window.

Insects were already investigating. The hole was large enough for a curious bird to enter. Or worse, I thought as I realized the sun was setting, a bat. We were going to need to cover the hole, at least until Jeff could contact his landlord. But how?

I searched the kitchen cabinets. Hadn't I seen—yes! At the top of one was a stack of paper plates. They were the perfect size.

Climbing on the counter, I grabbed a couple of them before rifling through Jeff's junk drawer. There had to be tape somewhere.

But it wasn't in the kitchen. Ignoring the fact that he couldn't be normal, I tried his bedroom. Sure enough, I found duct tape in his desk drawer.

I returned to the living room at the same time as Jeff. He sent me a confused look. "Everything okay?"

I help up my supplies. "Gonna tape up the window."

"With a plate?"

I shrugged. "You got anything better?"

"Nope. Let's try it."

The window was more tape than plate by the time we were done. But the hole was gone. I didn't have to worry about winged creatures entering during the night. With fresh drinks before us, we settled in to watch the rest of the game.

WHEN THE RED SOX FAILED TO SCORE THE TYING run in the bottom of the ninth, Jeff switched off the television and sent a wary glance toward the window. "I don't think we're going to get any more threats tonight, do you?"

I shook my head. "Hopefully not. Any idea who could have sent it?"

Jeff shrugged. "It's weird, isn't it? You find that link to the professor and an hour later someone's throwing a rock through the window?"

Biting my lip, I glanced around. "Your place isn't, like, bugged, is it?"

Jeff gave a nervous laugh. "I hope not. But, uh . . ." He eyed the window before turning back to me. "Just in case someone decides to . . . well . . . would you mind if I stayed in the bedroom tonight?"

I shrugged. "I guess I could sleep out here." But I didn't really want to. What if a flying creature broke my paper plate? Or someone tossed something else through the window?

Jeff shook his head. "No. I mean, okay, this is probably going to sound dumb, but I kind of don't want to sleep alone tonight." He gestured to the window.

I nodded. It hadn't bothered me before, but now that he said something, the thought of being alone *was* unsettling. "Yeah. I get it. You're totally welcome to stay in the bedroom."

Finally alone in her room, Stacey printed out all the transcripts she had scanned this week. There had to be a pattern.

She examined the first two off the printer. Both women were history majors. They had taken several of the same courses. They had a few others taught by the same professor.

With that in mind, Stacey picked up a third transcript. This girl had only taken one history class.

As Stacey read through the printouts, she realized one name was on every single page.

Courtney's words rang in Stacey's mind. An older man in the history department. If he cheated once, he would do it again. Could all these women have been having an affair with their professor? The same professor?

She ran to her computer. The school website had profiles on all its faculty, right? She clicked on the history department.

Only one person had been teaching for over thirty years. The same one whose name was on each of the transcripts. And who happened to be her advisor.

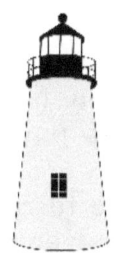

Chapter 11

I WAS RACING THROUGH AN OLD HOME, BEING chased by translucent bats and rats, when I heard a strange ringing sound. I turned to find the source.

And rolled against Jeff's chest. This felt nice. Smiling to myself, I snuggled a little closer.

But the ringing wouldn't stop. I cracked open an eye. It was still dark. The alarm clock on the side of the bed said it was just past four. Beside it was the source of the ringing: my cell.

I sat up quickly. Who would call at this hour? It had to be an emergency. All sorts of bad thoughts ran through my head as I fumbled for my phone. Had my brother been in an accident? Did something happen to my parents?

I didn't recognize the number, although the area code was from Connecticut. I flipped open the phone and accepted the call.

"Hello?"

"Katie? It's Todd."

"Todd?" My brain wasn't quite awake. Beside me, Jeff stirred as I tried to figure out if I knew anyone named Todd. The only person I could think of was—

"Yes. Todd. Your boss? You said you'd be back this weekend. It's the weekend. Where are you?"

I bit my lip. "I'm sorry. I completely forgot. I'm still in Maine. Things here are more complicated than I thought."

Todd's voice was seething. "Do you mean to tell me you're not coming in today?"

"No. I mean, yeah. I mean, I guess I just need a little more time here in Maine."

"And I need employees who are going to show up when they're supposed to. Obviously, that's not you. Spend as much time as you want in Maine. You're fired. Don't bother collecting your last paycheck. I'll put it in the mail."

Todd didn't wait for me to respond. I could hear him slam the phone on the receiver a moment before the call disconnected. As I folded my cell, I could feel tears in my eyes.

Jeff put a hand on the small of my back. "Everything okay?"

I shook my head, my voice wavering. "I . . . I was just fired." As I turned to Jeff, I could feel the tears streaming down my face, but I didn't care. "Now what am I going to do?"

Jeff sat up, pulling me close and letting me literally cry on his shoulder. "It'll be okay. It's not like you were going to work there forever, was it?"

I sniffed. "No, but it was a good job."

Jeff ran his hands in slow circles along my back. "Was it your dream job?"

I gave a small laugh. "I don't have a dream job. But this one paid the bills. Put food on the table. Paid my rent. If I don't find a new job, I'm going to have to sleep in my truck."

"That's not a truck. And things'll work out. I'm sure of it."

I wanted to believe him. Sitting there in his arms, I felt safe. I could trust whatever he told me.

I wanted to stay there forever, so I nuzzled a little closer. His hands continued moving up and down my back. As my tears subsided, I returned the gesture.

We stayed that way for a long time. I wasn't sure about Jeff, but I was completely comfortable. I could have continued like this forever.

But Jeff seemed to have another idea. Just the smallest amount of pressure changed his gentle caresses into something needier. Something I wanted as well.

As I continued to dance my fingers along his back, I tried to pull him closer. He obliged. When I turned my head slightly, his lips met mine. Or maybe mine were on his. Whoever started it, we were kissing each other.

His kiss was gentle. Sweet. And his hands never stopped moving. Pulling me closer. Making me crave him just a little more.

I leaned into him, gently lowering him onto the pillow. He pulled away, caressing my cheek as he smiled at me.

"What are we doing? I mean, are you okay with this? I'd hate to take advantage—"

I pressed a finger to his lips to silence him. "You're not taking advantage." With a smile, I straddled him, reaching into his nightstand. And I wasn't looking for a printout.

I WOKE UP FEELING MORE REFRESHED THAN I had in a while. I couldn't remember the last time I had slept so well. Not wanting to open my eyes, I snuggled into Jeff's chest.

Jeff's *bare* chest.

Oh no. I had slept with my best friend's brother. Lisa was going to kill me.

Not that I regretted it. Had he been anyone else, I probably would consider an encore before we crawled out of bed for brunch. But my best friend's brother? There were rules against that, weren't there?

Jeff didn't seem to know about them. He pulled me close, nuzzling his head into my hair. "Morning."

I rolled away, mumbling something that even I couldn't understand. Jeff didn't seem to be offended. He ran a hand along my hair. "You stay in bed. I'll go see what we have for breakfast."

Without waiting for an answer, he climbed out of the bed. I heard him rummage in the dresser for a moment before disappearing into the bathroom.

As I listened for the shower, I realized I had a few options. Most of my things were still in my bag. It wasn't like I had moved into Jeff's room. I could probably change and be in my car before he finished his shower.

But leaving would mean I would have to stop looking into Lisa's death. I had to be getting close enough for someone to be scared. Why else would someone threaten us last night?

How did anyone know we were getting close, though? That was the part that was still bothering me.

When the toilet flushed and the shower started running, I remembered my dilemma. Fleeing wasn't really an option. But what *was* normal behavior after a one-night stand? Ordinarily, I would consult Lisa. But, even if she were still alive, I wouldn't have been able to ask her.

I sighed. I was going to have to face my mistake like a big girl. Maybe if I didn't mention it, we could pretend nothing had happened. It was just a dream.

A fantastic dream. One of the best dreams of my life. One I would love to have again.

Shaking my head, I got out of bed. I had to clear my mind. And get dressed. I tore apart the bed, finally finding my pajamas at the foot of the bed, where the sheet tucked into the mattress. After hastily throwing them on, I made the bed and turned to my duffel bag.

I had a big problem. I had never intended to spend the entire week here. My choices were slim. I only had one bra and underwear left. My emergency pair. No more clean shirts. No more clean pants.

I glanced at the bag where I had been putting the clothes I had already worn. Yesterday's jeans were resting on the top. They weren't *that* dirty. I could probably get away with wearing them again. But what about a shirt? Despite my deodorant, I had been sweating all week. I didn't really want to wear any of those again.

I was still scowling at my bag when the bathroom door opened. Jeff emerged, carrying his dirty underwear to the hamper in his closet. He raised his eyebrows as he passed me.

"You okay?"

I shook my head. "What are the odds your building has a laundromat?"

"None. But there's one not that far. You need to wash something?"

"Yeah. Everything. I ran out of clothes. All I have left is one pair of underwear and yesterday's jeans."

Jeff couldn't quite manage to hide his smirk. I could only imagine what he was thinking. And I didn't need my mind going there right now. One problem at a time.

"Well, I suppose you *could* run around in your underwear. That might be interesting." Jeff opened a middle dresser drawer, rummaging a moment before tossing a shirt on the bed. "It might be a little big, but this should fit you."

"Thanks." I gestured toward the hall. "I'm going to go clean up."

Jeff nodded. "I'll make breakfast. Getting sick of eggs yet?"

"Sounds good to me."

"Awesome."

Jeff looked like he wanted to say something else. But I didn't let him. Before he could utter another word, I escaped to the bathroom.

JEFF GOT THE HINT. NEITHER OF US MENTIONED what had happened in the early hours of the morning. As he sat across from me at the dinette, he gestured to the living room window.

"So, I've been thinking about the whole baseball thing."

I frowned. "It makes no sense."

"Unless you were right about Rick."

"Huh?"

Jeff sighed. "Bear with me. So, let's assume there is a connection between Rick and all these girls. Like, an actual connection, not a coincidence. Let's also assume that Lisa left clues in her story. Well, then, wouldn't it make sense that Rick wouldn't want us reading Lisa's manuscript?"

I made a sour face. "I'm not sure I follow your logic. How would Rick even know I was reading it?"

Jeff shrugged. "We were talking about it in the truck yesterday when he was standing right outside. He could have overheard."

I sent him a skeptical look. "So, now what? Are you going to call that police officer?"

"And tell him what? That I think one of my colleagues threw a baseball through my window because I told him I was reading my sister's novel? No. I think the only way we're going to find out who sent that note is to figure out what happened to Lisa."

I bit into my toast. "Well, I need to do laundry today. So, that's a couple of hours sitting in the laundromat reading. I'm almost at the end."

Jeff sipped his coffee with a nod. "While you do that, I want to go talk to Phil."

"About the celebration thing?"

Jeff shook his head. "No. About this. My suspicions about Rick. He's known the man for a long time. I'd like to get his opinion."

I sent Jeff a wary look. "I'm not sure that's a good idea."

His expression was so full of pain, it practically broke my heart. "Katie, I need to know what happened to my sister. I really think he can help me."

"But what if he tells Rick what we suspect? Not malicious, but *you'll never guess what Jeff said. He thinks you're responsible for his sister's death. Isn't that crazy?* Even that could tip off Rick that we're on to him."

Jeff sighed. "I'll be careful. I can tell him I suspect someone. Someone I know. But I won't name names."

I pointed at him with my fork. "Then what's the point? You just said it was to get an idea of Rick."

Jeff threw his hands in the air, huffing back in exasperation. "I don't know. I just know that I need to get more information!"

"So, we finish reading the book."

Jeff leaned forward, raising his voice. "The book isn't real, Katie! That's a story that my sister imagined!"

I met him in the center of the table. "Based on things that really happened!"

Jeff shook his head. "These people mean nothing to you! They're random names. People you didn't even know existed a week ago. Maybe this is a game to you, but Lisa was my sister. I can't accept the fact that someone I know and trust is responsible for her death!"

Our faces were inches apart. But I didn't want to kiss him. I wanted to smack him. Instead, I stormed to my feet, knocking my chair to the floor. "How dare you suggest this is just a game! Lisa was my best friend! She was like a sister to me! I need to know how she died!"

I stormed to the bedroom, gathering my bag of laundry and my purse in one giant sweep. After checking I had my keys and phone, I added Lisa's manuscript to the pile and stormed to the apartment door. I glared through the kitchen. Jeff was still at the table. Were those tears in his eyes? I couldn't tell from this distance.

I slammed the door behind me as I left the apartment. He was wrong. Going to Phil wouldn't find us any answers. Lisa would tell help me learn what had happened to her.

I just better be right.

Stacey knew she had to hide. How could she have been so stupid? Professor North had opposed her project from the beginning. That should have been her first clue.

But no. She had let him read her rough draft. Now he knew about her research. Was she his next target?

What was she

OMG. He's here. If anyone reads this, I think I might be next!

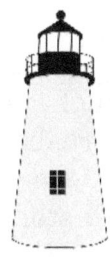

Chapter 12

I FURROWED MY BROWS AS I READ THE FINAL page of Lisa's manuscript. The last few sentences were so different from the rest of the story. It was also more difficult to read. It was almost like—

I sat upright, swearing loudly. A few people in the laundromat glanced my way, but I buried my head in the binder and they went back to their business.

My mind was reeling. Those last few lines weren't Lisa's story. They were a message from the author herself. Someone had found her. And killed her.

Her professor. Rick? Stacey's advisor hadn't liked her thesis. Did Lisa have that same problem with one of her own teachers?

I thought back to our conversations last year. It felt like forever ago. A professor in her department had been against her project. Did she ever tell me who?

I closed my eyes, listening to the rhythmic beat of the dryer behind me as I replayed the conversation. She had been surprised the professor was so against her idea, since it was a mixture of contemporary and historical fiction. Much like what he wrote.

The dryer signaled my laundry was done. But I hardly noticed. All I could hear was Lisa's voice. *He's probably going to reject anything I write unless it has witches in it.*

Phil hadn't liked her proposal! But what if it had nothing to do with the lack of witches? What if he had rejected it because he had been responsible for all the deaths she had uncovered?

And now Jeff was going to confront him! I had to stop him. As quickly as I could, I stuffed all my clothes into my bag while I scrolled through my phone book for Jeff's information. I hit send and rushed to my truck.

But the call went to voicemail. I knew he would recognize my number. I had stored it in his phone myself. Was he still mad at me from this morning? Or was he in trouble?

I had to get to Phil's house. My key was in the ignition when I realized I didn't know where I was going. I rushed back inside the laundromat. Hadn't I seen a pay phone in the corner of the room?

There was, but it didn't have a phone book. Biting my lip, I turned to the lady behind the counter. "Excuse me. Do you have a phone book I could borrow?"

The woman was old enough to be my grandmother. And I wasn't positive English was her first language. But she nodded. "Yes. Yes."

She rummaged under the counter before passing the phone book to me. I quickly flipped through the white pages, slowing when I reached the N's. *Norton. Norton.* I traced my finger down the page.

> Norton, Penelope
> Norton, Peter
> Norton, Phineas
> Norton, Phoebe

Phil wasn't listed. Now what? Gnawing at my lip, I considered my options.

I could call information, but in my experience, they couldn't usually find anyone not listed in the phone book.

I could search the online white pages. But I needed the internet. Where could I go? Not back to Jeff's place. I didn't have his keys. I'd never get into the building, nevermind the apartment.

The library probably had internet access. Where was it? Hadn't I seen it while we were driving yesterday? I closed my eyes and tried to picture it. Hadn't it been near the green where we were touring the landmarks? Could I get there myself? I had to try.

I peeled out of the parking lot, following signs for Historic Kensington. As I approached, I saw the street sign with the guy reading a book. The arrow pointed down a road to my left. A few minutes later, I had parked across two spaces and was running into the library.

I went straight to the reference desk. "Hi. I need to use a computer. I just need to look up something quick."

The librarian pointed to three monitors beneath the window on my right. "Those are for under ten minutes. Just type *guest* in the username."

"Thanks so much."

I made a beeline for the one in the center. After logging in as a guest, I waited for the home screen to load. It felt like forever. Every second wasted here was one that Jeff could be in trouble. Was I worried because he was my best friend's brother? Or because we had slept together?

Opening an internet browser, I shook my head. He was a friend. That was why I was worried.

I found the white pages easily enough, typing in *Phil Norton*. I assumed it was short for Philip. But I wasn't sure if he had one or two l's. For all I knew, his name could be Phillippe or Philbert. He didn't spell it with an F, did he?

The results popped onto my screen. There were three Philip Nortons in the Kensington area. Only one did not have a wife listed. I scribbled the address on a scrap of paper between the two computers, then headed to MapQuest.

Phil lived near the ocean. I copied the directions, being sure to log out of the computer when I finished. As I started the car, I glanced at the clock. I had only been in the library for ten minutes. It had felt like hours.

When I turned onto Phil's street, I realized I didn't really have a plan. Should I just knock on the door? If Jeff was still mad at me, he wouldn't be thrilled to see me. But if Phil was trying to kill him, he'd be ecstatic I was there.

Unless Phil hurt me, too. Then neither of us would be very happy.

I passed Phil's house. Jeff's truck was parked in front. So, he was there. That was a start. I drove past a few more houses before turning around on a side street and passing Phil's again.

I parked two doors down, but I still didn't have a plan. Knocking wouldn't work. I needed to try something else.

As I reached the property line, I crouched low, following a copse of trees toward the backyard. It wasn't big, but it was thick enough to provide me with cover. I couldn't see the house, so I doubted anyone could see me.

Unfortunately, that also meant I couldn't see what was going on. I crept to the edge of the copse, standing inside the flowing branches of an elderberry bush. It was a perfect hiding place. I pushed aside just enough of the plant to peek through.

It wasn't obvious from the street, but the copse was only a car's length away from the house. I could easily see right through an open window. And the sight had me freezing in fear.

Jeff was tied to an armchair. His head was drooping, but I watched as it moved from one shoulder to the other. He was still alive.

Phil was pacing the room in front of Jeff, his back to me. He was too far away for me to know whether he was saying something or just walking off nervous energy. I needed to get closer.

I watched for at least a minute, but Phil never turned in my direction. Steeling my nerves, I rushed to the window, squatting in the bushes as close to the house as I could get. While I waited for my heart to stop racing, I tried to listen to what was happening inside.

Someone was mumbling. Was it Phil? I couldn't tell. I strained a little harder.

"I never wanted it to come to this."

A second voice responded. "What's going on?"

That was definitely Jeff. I needed help. What could I do? Maybe if I tried to call him again, Phil would answer and I could—what? Lure him out of the house somehow?

I couldn't do that near the window. Phil might hear me. I crept along the bushes until I reached the back of the house, then ran to the copse. Squatting behind a maple, I dug through my pockets. Where was my phone?

Not there. All I found were some quarters and a business card. But where was my phone? Probably still in my car. Hunching low, I ran along the trees. As soon as I reached the road, I stood, sprinting the rest of the way to the car.

My cell was on the front seat. And I hadn't bothered locking the door. I grabbed the phone and immediately dialed 9-1-1. But the call wouldn't connect.

I tried again, and again it wouldn't go through. Now what?

The business card was still in my hand. I frowned at it. Where did I get this?

From the police officer last night. He *had* said to call him if we had new information. Phil tying up Jeff counted as new information, right? Fumbling with the card, I quickly punched in the numbers. Then I held my breath as I waited for the officer to answer.

One ring.

Two rings.

Three rings.

Oh no. It was going to go straight to voicemail.

"Hello? This is Officer Carson."

"Hi. M-my name is K-Katie Winters. W-We had the baseball in the, in the window last night. My friend, my friend is being held hos-hostage. I think it's the same guy that, that threw the baseball."

The officer sighed. "Where are you?"

"36 Sea Cliff Lane."

"What town?"

It never occurred to me he might be in another town. "K-Kensington."

"Okay. I'll send someone over."

He ended the call, and I shoved the phone into my back pocket. I needed to check on Jeff. Was Phil going to kill him?

I crept back to the side of the house. I could still see Jeff in the window. He wasn't moving. Had Phil killed him?

Where *was* the professor, anyway? I couldn't see him. Had he gone into another room?

Before I could sidestep to get a better look, something collided with my temple. As I turned around, I saw Phil glowering at me from the other side of the bush. Then my world went black.

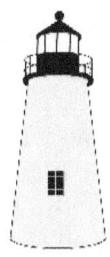

Chapter 13

"KATIE!"

Why was Jeff yelling at me? Were we still in bed? His arms were around me. I probably wouldn't have minded, but I didn't like that he was pinning my arms to my side. And my head hurt. How much had we drunk last night?

I tried to roll away, but I couldn't move. Panicked, I opened my eyes.

I wasn't in bed. I was in a chair next to Jeff. My arms were tied to it, but my hands and legs were free. I was pretty sure that information was useful, but my head hurt too much to think how.

Jeff and I were alone in the room. He was looking at me, his expression a mixture of fear and confusion. Basically, how I was feeling at that moment.

But when I spoke, I tried to keep my voice calm and steady. "Jeff? What's going on?"

"I'm not sure. I was telling Phil about my concerns about Rick, but I was being vague about who I suspected."

I gasped. "He must have thought you suspected him."

"But why would he think that?"

"I think he did it. I don't really know why, though."

Phil's voice answered us from the doorway. "Because she wanted to tell the police."

Jeff and I both turned to face our captor. He shook his head mournfully. "I didn't want to hurt her. I kept trying to get her to change her story. But she was so determined."

I glared at him. "She knew you had killed all those girls. Made them look like accidents or suicides so no one would suspect you."

Phil nodded. "I knew she was getting close. She kept telling me she had writer's block, but I was pretty sure she was avoiding me. Then, she ups and leaves campus in the middle of the semester. That's when I knew she had figured out it was me."

"You went to see her."

Jeff whipped his head in my direction. "He what? How do you know?"

The lump in my throat made it difficult to utter the words. "Lisa never stopped writing her story. She was writing it that day. At the bottom of the page, she scribbled you were there. She worried you were going to kill her."

Phil threw up his hands in exasperation. "I never *meant* to kill her. She wasn't a Hannah."

Jeff raised his eyebrows. "A Hannah? Like, Hannah Cooper?"

"Yes. I told you yesterday. Hannah Cooper is still alive. Her spirit passes from one girl to the next."

"That's ridiculous!"

Phil shook his head adamantly. "That's what your sister said. But Hannah killed the love of my life."

Phil looked ready to hurt us. But the police were on their way. How long had I been unconscious? Shouldn't they be here by now? Even if the officer hadn't been in Kensington—

I gulped. Phil didn't live in Kensington. There had been a sign just before I had turned onto the road. I had crossed the border into Littleneck. The police would never find us now.

Jeff and I were on our own. I leaned forward slightly in my chair. Did my ropes give a little? It was probably my imagination, but I wasn't about to abandon hope.

I also couldn't let Phil see me trying to free myself. At the moment, he was too busy pacing the room to notice me. My best bet was to keep him talking.

I tried to keep my voice calm. "How?"

When Phil turned his attention to me, I could see a crazed look in his eye. I had no doubt he was going to kill me. But at least he didn't seem to be in a rush to do so.

"How what?"

"Your . . . love. How did she die?"

Phil's eyes filled with a far-away look. "Did you know I'm a direct descendant of Hetty Norton? My whole life, I was told about what that witch had done. How she was still living. And then, one day, I met her."

"How'd you know she was Hannah Cooper?"

Phil waved a dismissive hand. "I didn't. Not at first. My senior year of college, my fiancée started acting strange. She was a student at Down East and I would visit her on the weekend. At first, I thought it was just the stress of school. But then one weekend, she told me that her roommate was a witch that was out to kill her. She died in my arms just as the witch came back into the room. See, Hannah had heard her and killed her."

I could see Jeff didn't believe Phil any more than I did, but his voice was neutral when he spoke. "Did you tell the police?"

"The police. They did nothing. Said Victoria had a bad acid trip. Let Hannah get away. So, I went back to the dorm late one night. Told Hannah Victoria had something she wanted me to give her, but it had to be from the roof. When we got there, I pushed her. Everyone thought she killed herself, distraught over her roommate's death."

I frowned. "When was that? I never saw that when we were researching deaths at the university."

Phil smirked. "Not as good as your friend. She went all the way back to 1965. Victoria's death was the story that inspired her to have her own story be about drugs."

Jeff looked disgusted. "So, you've been killing random women for nearly forty years?"

Phil smacked Jeff across the face with the back of his hand. "They weren't random. Weren't you listening? I knew that killing Hannah wasn't enough. She would come back. So, I got a job at the university. Kept an eye on the students, since Hannah rarely moved far from home. I even volunteered to work with the new student orientation to try to find her at the beginning of the semester."

I bit my lip. "How did you know if a student was Hannah?"

Phil shooed away my question. "I learned to spot the signs. I watched them for a while. Sometimes, I would sit in on their introductory classes, watching to see if they were scoping new victims."

I wanted to be sick. "You stalked them?"

Phil shook his head. "No, no. Just watched them. Invited them to my office under the pretense of making sure they were adjusting. But really, I was asking questions I knew only a witch could answer. When I was convinced I found the next Hannah Cooper, I found different ways of making her death look like a suicide. Always figured out the how before I even tried to kill her. That's the key, you know. I needed to perform my vanquishing ritual to keep Hannah away longer."

"And no one ever figured out it was you?"

Phil shrugged.

Jeff looked as ill as I felt. But when he spoke, his voice was full of anger. "So, what? You thought my sister was a witch, too?"

Phil shook his head. "You don't listen, do you? No. I knew she wasn't a Hannah. I had no intention of killing her. I'm not a murderer."

I could name at least sixteen women who would disagree with him, but I thought it best not to mention them. Instead, I tried to get Phil to continue his story. "So, what happened?"

He sighed. "It was an accident. When she left school, I figured she went home. I found her address in her student records and went to visit her. She wouldn't even open the door. Threatened to call the police."

Jeff glared at our captor. "So, you killed her?"

"No! I just went around the back, found an open window, and climbed inside. She was still in the living room. When she saw me, she screamed. I didn't want the neighbors to hear, so I hit her. I just meant to quiet her, but she fell. Hit her head on the corner of the table."

I had thought knowing the truth about what happened to Lisa would make me feel better. Instead, it was like she had died all over again. I could barely see Phil through my tears.

He didn't seem to notice. It was as if he *wanted* to tell us what had happened. "I thought I killed her. She wouldn't wake up. I didn't know what to do. As I loaded her into my car, I saw a bicycle near the garage. I took that too. Brought her to that lighthouse she was always talking about. It was late, and no one was there. I almost killed myself carrying her out onto the jetty."

Phil was pacing faster, his words tumbling out. "We were almost at the end when she stirred. I swear. I didn't realize she was still alive."

Jeff's words were venomous. "But you killed her, anyway."

"I had no choice! She was going to turn me in. She didn't understand!"

"What makes you think we do?"

I turned to Jeff, unable to stop the tears leaking down my face. "He doesn't. He's going to kill us next."

Phil looked at us imploringly. "It's not like I *want* to. You didn't give me any choice."

Jeff scowled. "Then why haven't you done it yet?"

"I told you. I can't just *murder* anyone. I need a plan. It has to look like an accident."

My brain started racing with dozens of ways he could kill me. Each was more horrific than the last.

But instead of imagining the multitude of ways I could die, I tried to focus on a scenario that would allow me to live. My arms weren't getting any looser, but Phil was so lost in thought, he wasn't even looking at me.

I only had one chance, and not much of a plan.

Channeling every action movie I had ever watched, I lunged forward in my chair, planting my feet on the ground and turning as quickly as possible.

The chair smacked Phil hard enough to knock him to his knees, but it didn't break as I had hoped. While the crazy professor uttered a litany of creative insults, I jumped on him, chair first, in my best backward imitation of a pro wrestler.

This time, the chair splintered. It wasn't much, but it was enough to free myself from my ropes. As I struggled to my feet, I could see Phil lying motionless on the floor. Blood was pooling beside his head.

My vision blurred, and I thought I was going to be sick. Had I *killed* him?

"Katie!"

Jeff's voice snapped me back to the current situation. I rushed to untie him. Thankfully, that meant I wouldn't have to see Phil's lifeless body.

"Katie. Are you okay?"

I took a shaky breath. "Not really. Ugh. My hands are shaking. I can't break these knots."

"Stand back."

Jeff got to his feet, much like I had. But instead of slamming against Phil, he ran into the nearest wall, splintering his chair with his first try. As soon as he freed himself, he grabbed my hand. "Come on. Let's get out of here before he wakes up."

I gulped. "He's dead."

"Oh, you think so, huh?"

We both turned to the voice. Phil stood in the middle of the room, blood dripping down his face as he pointed his gun at us. His smile matched the crazy expression in his eyes.

Jeff released my hand, shifting his weight just enough to block me from Phil's gun. "Katie. Get out of here. Find help."

But I was frozen in fear.

Phil smirked. "Oh please. Go get help. It won't matter. I'll still find you. By the time the police get here, you'll both be dead."

I found my voice. "They'll still charge you with our murders."

"Not if I shoot Jeff in self-defense. The poor, deranged boy. He killed his parents, you know. When his sister found out, he killed her. You came to tell me your suspicions, but he followed you. Killed you, right here in my living room. When he tried to shoot me, I wrestled away this gun and shot him."

Phil sounded so convincing, I almost believed him. Jeff looked as confused as I felt. But Jeff wasn't the murderer. Phil was. One look in his eyes was enough to remind me.

Again, I acted without thinking. In a motion so fast that I startled myself, I picked up the remains of Jeff's chair and heaved it at Phil. Grabbing Jeff's hand, I ran outside.

The professor was on our tail. I raced to the copse of trees on the border. It wasn't much, but maybe it would be dense enough to block Phil's shooting.

As I reached the nearest tree, I heard the distant wail of police sirens. It was punctuated by gunshots. I ducked behind the largest trunk I could find.

Where was Jeff? I had lost his hand as soon as we had left the house. Had he followed me? Or were those shots aimed at him?

Swallowing my fear, I closed my eyes and tried to filter the surrounding sounds. The sirens had stopped. There were a lot of voices, but I couldn't discern any of them.

A new sound broke the silence. Branches breaking. Had Jeff found me?

Slowly, I peered around the tree. It wasn't Jeff. It was Phil!

But he didn't see me. He was looking toward the house. Walking backward as he pointed the gun in the direction of the sirens. That was stupid. He could trip on something. Like that big branch sitting between us.

A horrible idea popped into my head. Without really thinking about what I was doing, I lunged for the branch.

My intention was to jump to my feet and clock Phil in the head before he knew what was happening. But the branch was heavier than I expected. I struggled to stand. And gave Phil plenty of time to see that I was behind him.

As he turned toward me, I held the branch like a baseball bat, channeled the memories of my horrible middle school gym classes, and swung. The branch hit Phil in the thigh, throwing him off balance. As he fell to my right, I dodged to my left.

A gunshot broke the silence. It sounded so loud in the stillness of the trees. It was quickly followed by shouting and more rushing footfalls, all growing louder.

But I couldn't dwell on what I was hearing. I had to get away from Phil. Turning my back on the crazy professor, I ran for my life. I made it two steps before my foot caught on a rock and I tumbled forward.

Crawling on my hands and knees, I glanced over my shoulder as I scrambled away. Phil wasn't moving. Why not? Was he playing possum? Or had he hit his head on a rock?

Curiosity overrode my common sense. I stopped running away. From my perch on the ground, I saw police officers rushing into the copse. One of them nearly tripped over Phil. Another pointed his gun at me.

"Don't move."

Did raising my hands count as moving? I slowly placed them in the air as I had seen on television. "Don't shoot. I was just trying to get away from Phil."

Before the officer could react, Jeff rushed to me. "Katie!" He pulled me close. All the fear of the past few hours drained away as I sank into him. He stroked my hair. "You're okay."

Nodding, I stepped back and glanced at our attacker. Officers were surrounding him, so I couldn't see. I returned my attention to Jeff. "What about Phil? Is he . . ." I swallowed hard.

The officer that had been ready to shoot me a moment ago shook his head. "No. He'll live."

Jeff turned to the officer. "He killed my sister. And so many other women."

I still couldn't see Phil, but I could hear him from the ground. "I had to. Hannah Cooper. She just won't leave me alone."

The officers shook their heads at each other, sharing looks that clearly indicated they thought Phil was crazy. As they helped him to his feet, his hands cuffed behind his back, I caught my final glimpse of the man who had killed my best friend.

Was he crying?

ELEVEN
MONTHS
LATER

Stacey looked across the courtroom at the man standing before the judge. Nineteen consecutive life sentences. Even if they were to be served in the asylum, at least Professor North would never hurt anyone again.

It wouldn't bring back her friend. But, thankfully, no more innocent lives would be lost.

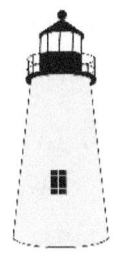

Epilogue

I LOOKED UP FROM MY COMPUTER WHEN I HEARD the knock on my open door. Jeff smiled at me from across my classroom.

"Ready to go home?"

I nodded. "Yup. Just submitted my final grades."

As I shut down my computer, Jeff entered the room, resting against one of the desks in the front row. He held up a paperback. "Look what Rick sent me."

My eyes went wide as I drew closer. "Is that Lisa's book?" I took it from his hands, turning it over slowly a few times.

He nodded, tears in his eyes. "Rick edited it and published it for her. But I thought it was unfinished."

I bit my lip. "I wanted to surprise you. I mean, I'm nowhere near as good a writer as Lisa, but Rick helped me."

Jeff frowned. "I thought he creeped you out."

I sighed. "He used to. But we met at the university coffee shop and other public places until he grew on me."

Jeff kissed my forehead. "I read the last chapter. Thank you. It means a lot to me that you did this."

Tears were forming in my own eyes. "I did it for me, too, you know."

"I know." He stood, putting an arm around me. "Ready to go home?"

I returned to my desk. "I think so."

"So you made it through your first year at Kensington High. Did you sign your contract for next year?"

I held the form in the air. "On one condition. We spend the summer in Copper Cove. The apartment is getting so cramped."

Jeff brought his face close to mine. "Deal."

He sealed it with a kiss. And in my heart, I knew Lisa approved.

Did you like this story?

Join my newsletter to learn about other new releases.
https://ashleighstevens.eo.page/whodunit

As a thank you, you'll receive a FREE copy of

Kayaks
Kisses
&
Monsters

**A summer of kayaking sounds perfect.
Until the lake monster appears.**

For Ellie, getting paid to spend her summer outside sounds like the ideal internship, even if it means paddling up and down a river twelve hours a day. Sure, she's never actually been in a kayak before, but how hard could it be?

At least she knows how to set up camp at night. Unlike her co-worker. Though Clay may be captain of the crew team, she could teach him a thing or two about spending the night in a sleeping bag.

And then there's the whole lake monster thing. Of course, Ellie knows water monsters aren't real but Clay doesn't seem convinced, especially after a boater goes missing. When mysterious accidents threaten her job security, Ellie starts to wonder why the "monster" wants her gone.

One Night in Sedona

Who would have thought that a single photograph would be so dangerous?

Photofest. The ultimate photography convention. Not only is Seddy finally able to attend, but this year, it is being held in the city for which she was named. And she cannot wait.

No sooner does she check into the conference when a murder interrupts her night on the town with a new friend. Shaken, Seddy just wants to put the incident behind her.

But someone has other ideas. After attending her first day of workshops, Seddy discovers her hotel room has been ransacked. Her new love interest seems very eager to help her while the local detective keeps asking her questions about her camera. To make matters worse, the chief of police keeps giving her strange looks.

And then someone tries to kill her.

As she works out whom she can trust, Seddy realizes she may hold the one piece of evidence that could help solve the mystery.

Now Available

About the Author

Once upon a time, there was a girl who loved reading and learning so much that she wanted to share her writing with others. She wrote her first novella at twelve-years-old, although it has never been published. She continued writing for the next twenty years, developing a writing style and finding a comfortable genre.

In 2010, just before the birth of her first child, Ashleigh decided to publish her first novel. Not long after, Ashleigh decided to become a stay-at-home mother in order to spend time with her daughter and continue her writing.

Currently, Ashleigh lives in Southern Connecticut with her husband and her four beautiful children, whom she homeschools. In her spare time, Ashleigh continues working on her novels, hoping to publish more soon.

Read more at www.AshleighStevensBSB.com

Other Works by Ashleigh Stevens

<u>Young Adults</u>
Camp Piquaqua
Elephant on my Chest

<u>Hartfield Chronicles</u>
Lesson 0: A New Home
Lesson 1: Adjusting to a New Life
Webserial

<u>Romances</u>
Kayaks, Kisses & Monsters
Mooncrossed

<u>Mysteries</u>
PS: It Was Murder
One Night In Sedona (writing as Carrie Latimer)

To receive updates on new releases, visit
www.AshleighStevensBSB.com
or join my newsletter
https://ashleighstevens.eo.page/whodunit